Parallel Paths

MARGARET SWINDELL

First published 2008 by
MS Publications
Jesmond
Newcastle upon Tyne

Copyright © 2008 Margaret Swindell

This book is a work of fiction.
Names and characters are the product
of the author's imagination and any
resemblance to actual person's living
or dead, is entirely coincidental.

All rights reserved. No part of this publication
may be reproduced, stored in a retrieval system,
or transmitted, in any form or by any means,
electronic, mechanical, photocopying, recording
or otherwise, without the prior permission of the author.

ISBN 978-0-9559106-0-9

Printed and bound in Great Britain

Part 1

Chapter 1

'And now we beseech the Great Architect of the Universe.....'
The declamatory tones drifted down the staircase. Harold Hunt, dark, balding, was rehearsing his latest speech, for the ears of his Masonic brethren. At noon he was usually starting his lunch. It would be a heavy affair of meat, potatoes and greens, with a custardy sweet to follow. Today his meal wasn't ready. This break in his routine was becoming all too common since the birth of his twins. His annoyance approached anger as he thought of the continual crying of the babes. They caused him sleepless nights and on the part of his wife Edna, an inability to cope. If it wasn't for his mother, he didn't know how they would manage.

In her kitchen, Edna was making a pie. As she rubbed fat into flour for the pastry, her mind was far off. She saw the bright image of a cruise ship. Its red funnels poured out steam. New paint gleamed on its steep hull. Women in headbands and plunging waistlines played deck tennis with their men. In the streamlined bar, the cocktails flowed. She and Harold had been booked on such a cruise. It had been cancelled when she got pregnant with the twins. She saw herself in one of the cabins, laying out her cream satin nightie. Harold had put out his red Moroccan slippers, with their matching case. Thrust back into reality by Harold's Masonic drone, Edna put the pie in the oven. In the nearby porch, Harold's mother rocked the sleeping twins.

Some time later, Harold finished his diatribe. He left the room, shouting down the stairs as he ran,
'Edna, for Christ's sake get that dinner out!'

He entered the dining room and sat at the head of the table, drumming his fingers on its cloth. His daughters Lulu and Bonnie were seated already. Lulu, his eldest, was a typist. Dark, attractive, her thoughts were on boyfriend Larry, as she waited. Bonnie, bobbed head looked down at her plate. Why didn't Mum hurry, she thought. She'd be late for school. Then son Osbert and their grandmother came in. The twins were still asleep in the porch. Sandy haired Osbert, eighteen, had recently left his Quaker boarding school.

Calming down, satisfaction spread over Harold's face as he looked around. The mantelpiece, with turquoise tiles and Corinthian columns, framed the fire's glow. Rather too large for his modest home, it was one of the pieces he had picked up from sale rooms. An Indian red suite faced the fire, its carved wood heavy with fruit. Tasselled lamps echoed its tones. The geometric wallpaper in shades of beige was Edna's choice. Harold's heavy brows met in a frown as he thought of giving in to her views. A mahogany sideboard was heavy with ornaments. Harold loved them, the Marley horses, a dusky couple with grapes and a glass domed centrepiece. These ancient objects were his mother's and he allowed no change.

As her husband's angry tones burst into the kitchen, Edna's dreamlike expression changed. Clumsily dropping a spoon, she rushed into the dining room to face the assembled hoard. Harold, siblings and grandmother, attempted to quiet the now bawling twins. Edna, Marcel waves rumpled, put down her concoction on its waiting mat. She burst into tears as reality dawned. The pastry covered pie was large enough only for two!

The tiny pie grew cold beside carrots and mash. Harold's stern mother tried to comfort them all. Her grey hair was screwed into a bun, her patterned dress long. It had a high neck such as Queen Alexandra wore. Harold questioned her
'What's been going on that led to this? Why wasn't I told?'
Well Lad, you just didn't notice. Edna's been staring into space for weeks. She leaves me to feed the babies most days and I can't bottle feed

both of them at once! You complain enough about their crying!'

Harold's slippered feet hurried towards the phone.

'Come in Doctor Anderson' called the grandmother, ushering him into the cold drawing room.

No-one had switched on the Magicole fire.

'Have a seat Doctor' Harold said, explaining the lunch time fiasco.

His mother brought Edna in. The G.P.'s face loomed close as he asked 'Now Mrs Hunt, tell me how you've been feeling.'

Edna, terrified, said little in answer to his questions.

'I'm afraid your wife's had a breakdown Mr Hunt.' he said to Harold.

'She'll have to go away, unless a room could be used here, with a nurse.'

Harold, mindful of the little used drawing room, looked at his grim faced mother. Recalling its parties with laughing guests when his father was alive, he knew she would never agree. Though wanting it for Edna, he hadn't the courage to say so. He vetoed the prospect.

'In that case,' the doctor continued 'I suggest she goes in as a voluntary patient. Ideally she could leave if she wished.'

Harold agreed on a Yorkshire Dales hospital, though worried about doing the wrong thing. Their grandmother calmed down the family.

'What's to be done about the babies?' Harold asked, with a hesitance shown only to his mother.

'Don't look at me Lad' she snapped, 'I've done my whack, but I'll ask around for a foster mother.'

During the car journey to the remote retreat, Edna's tears were unavailing. Parking by the roadside for a last picnic, she smiled. Tears threatened again when she brought out cups just for two. They looked lost on the bright check cloth, so often spread with a huge family meal. Scarcely able to eat, she began crying again as she repacked the basket. Her pleas became desperate,

'Please please, don't send me away Harold!' As she broke down.

Harold swerved, as his hand flew up to wipe away a tear of his own.

He felt relieved when soon she fell into an exhausted sleep.

Setting off that morning, he had driven the Red Peril, his son's smart two seater. He sensed that the journey might seem less traumatic than if he used his severe black Austin. The October sun had seemed warm. He had left down the hood, and the cold now penetrated, intensifying his grief.

He regretted not getting help for Edna sooner. His mother had hinted at problems, but he had seen these as women's concern. Away at his office all day, it was only hearsay to him. Apparently the twins cried for so long they stopped breathing, kinking his mother called it. When their doctor diagnosed convulsions, he felt he had made the right move for Edna.

As he drove, Harold recalled the fresh young girl Edna had been when they met. He'd been scarcely able to speak for longing, when seeing her home from chapel. One Saturday afternoon, he'd taken her on the river that watered the Huddersfield mills. As he rowed, the blackening stone of terraces gave way to cottages around courtyards. At length there was only sun drenched green, wooded hills, fields and farms with their scattered barns. He had moored the boat and hand in hand they had crept up the bank. They had lain in a hollow dappled with sun and heavy with the scent of crushed wild plants..... They'd been quiet on the way home. Edna had gazed at her stained white dress and her straw hat's broken flowers.

Since Harold's marriage at nineteen to pregnant Edna, the quiet of his home had seemed oppressive. An only child, he had always been glad to get away. He wondered now how deep the place's gloom had seemed to Edna, torn from a house full of siblings. Then Louisa arrived to lighten their lives. Pampered by parents and grandparents alike, she was vivacious almost from birth.

'Little Lulu!' her grandfather had christened her, as she sat flirtatiously on his knee.

After two years Osbert was born and seven years later, Barbara called Bonnie.

Although Edna had never regained the wild joy of their day on the river, she had seemed happy enough. Harold had thought so until the birth of the twins. He could only blame the event on himself. He'd forgotten to order more contraceptives (carefully sent, 'under plain cover'). He had confounded matters by double ports and lemon, at one of his Masonic nights out. The hazy pleasure, so quickly over, was scarcely worth what had followed. If only the twins had been boys. They might have been thankful to inherit his business, unlike their brother Osbert.

Harold had anxieties about property too. He kept his eyes open for council plans, possibly affecting his shops. He might make good money by selling off the land. There was also the worry of the right of light. Barker, the tailor who had this right, was a fellow Freemason. Harold tried to sweeten him by ordering suits, but would Barker hold up a sale despite this? Harold might have to pay up. Still, with the number of bankruptcies around, it was as well he had fingers in so many pies. At the word 'pies' he was swiftly recalled to the present.

Fast moving clouds were gathering, when stark against the bright horizon appeared the long low buildings with their monstrous towers. As heavy drops fell on the open car, Edna wakened. She saw with dismay, a vast complex. Each unit vied in menace with its neighbour in the deepening gloom. Thoroughly soaked, her last cries of

'Turn back, Harold! Please turn back!' had to be ignored.

Heavily starched bodies surrounded a trembling Edna and marched her through an echoing hall. Their feet clattered up flight after flight of stairs, unlocking and locking doors as they went. Snatches of sound, more animal than human, reinforced Edna's mounting dread. Later that evening, in a striped cotton night-dress under cold sheets, she cried until she slept.

Harold, having dispatched the formalities, put up his car hood and began the drive home. A gnawing guilt clouded the journey. After stopping for a pub meal, it was late when he reached Windsor Drive. The street was in darkness except for his home's bright windows. He decided to garage the car later and ran through the slanting rain. His spirits rose as the doorway bathed him in the jewel glow of the stair post lamp.

'Come in Lad,' said his mother, leading the way into the sitting room. 'I've just made a fresh pot of tea, would you like some?'

'I would that!' answered Harold, thawing beside the welcoming blaze, as his mother handed him tea and scones. Her face close to his, grey hair straying from its bun, she queried

'Well how did it all go Lad?'

'I hope to God I've done the right thing Mother' he said.

'Are you sure she was bad enough for that Bedlam? I'd shoot myself if I thought we'd put her there for nothing.

He put down his plate, unable to eat.

'She couldn't go on like that, what else could we do?' his mother went on.

'Anyway Harold, I've found a foster mother for the twins. A Mrs Chapel, a mother with a single daughter. She seems motherly, the daughter loves children, why don't we give it a try?'

'I'm not sure Mother. Couldn't you manage them, if Lulu gave up her job? Anyhow, I'll see to it in the morning.'

At six a.m. Edna woke to the clanging of trolleys. Her despairing slowness exasperated the nurses.

'Get a move on!' said one, anxious to get ready for breakfasts.

In contrast, the inmates' days were empty, except for the endless circling of thought. Expecting to see her own clothes, Edna had to take what was given, carbolic smelling garments from a trolleyed heap. The staff then sat their charges round a dayroom, like wallflowers at a partnerless dance.

As the day idled on, Edna felt trapped. Angrily she stared at the highly polished floor. How could Harold have brought her here?, she thought. He couldn't have cared for her at all. She'd never have married him if she hadn't got pregnant with Lulu. What a fool she'd been! Furiously she plucked at her skirt. Why, she could have had a dressmaking business, apprenticed as she was at thirteen. Look at her friend Miss Broom. Sewing made her a good living and her money was all her own!

'Time for toileting! jump to it!' a nurse shouted.

Grabbing Edna's arm, she rushed her to the toilet, standing beside her throughout.

The padding of ward shoes announced lunch. An odour of overcooked cabbage swept through with the unlocking of doors. Edna whispered to her neighbour

'Does it taste as bad as it smells?'

The woman didn't answer, lost in her own dream world. As the patients ambled to the dining hall, a wave of guilt broke over Edna. She should have been grateful not to live like some families Harold saw. He had come in one lunch time too sick to eat.

'What's the matter Love!' she had asked.

'I was canvassing and a woman asked me in. As I drank a mug of tea, something landed 'plop' on my hat. I looked up and the ceiling was crawling with bugs! I was out like a shot I can tell you!'

Nearing the food, Edna was sickened by its smell, but she took a tray and began eating. She recalled the cancellation of their Mediterranean cruise. On finding her pregnant, Harold had vetoed the trip.

'It was being landed with twins, instead of the cruise, that put me in here.' she muttered. No one reacted, as she broke the silence.

Back at Windsor Drive, Lulu was changing the twins' nappies. Their cries filled the room until one of them suddenly stopped.

'Grandma, she's kinking!' Lulu cried, rushing to get the child's bottom on the sink.

The shock of the cold porcelain caused a gasp and breathing began again. Cora, now in her grandmother's arms, fed slowly through a tiny hole in her bottle's teat. Cathy, the heavier, was usually fed last. Her cries rasped with anger, waiting through Cora's slow feeds. She then fed greedily through a large holed teat.

Lulu was anxious to get back to work. Continuing her typing job hadn't been easy.

'You'll give up that job and help your Grandmother!' Harold had raged.

'They're not my kids!' she had countered. 'I won't stay at home and be an old maid!'

She wouldn't give in, though Harold stormed. He took the decision to foster.

After the fresh air of the park, the twins were now asleep, one at each end of their large twin pram. The prospective fosterers, Mrs Chapel and her daughter, took a peep at the babies.

'Aren't they bonny!' the elder woman whispered.

'Eeh Mam they're lovely!' said her daughter.

They were soon sitting in the drawing room, warming as the electric fire glowed. Mrs and Miss Chapel faced questions from Harold and his mother. The older woman, a former nurse, seemed kind and capable. The daughter's face with its black currant eyes smiled, but Harold felt a disquiet.

'There was something about the younger woman I couldn't quite take to.....What do you think mother?'

'There was something severe about her' answered his mother 'but after all she's no beauty.'

Harold gave in. The couple fostered the twins for two years.

Chapter 2

The twins were lying one at each end of a large cot. Harold laid a toy beside each child, spotted dogs, one green one yellow. They reacted little to the stimulus.

'The poor little buggers look miserable.' he thought, noticing their turn down corner mouths.

He remembered guiltily wishing them away at their birth two years earlier. Not wanting to baby talk, he left as the foster mother cooed

'Look at the bow-wows!'

His shoulders straightened as he strode into the keen fresh air.

He had set off early to drive to the Dales to see Edna, buying chrysanthemums in a brilliant yellow. Driving off in his sober black Austin, there was a sharpness in the September air. As he approached the hospital buildings now grimly familiar, he heaved himself out of his car. Locking it he moved up the steps, lethargic at the futility of the visit.

Edna had neither smiled nor spoken to Harold for at least six months. Seated as usual against the walls of the bleak room, with nothing to do, she didn't even turn her head when he pulled up a chair.

'Hope you like these Love.' he said, handing her the
flowers. 'A nice cheerful colour I thought.'

They didn't cheer Edna. She pushed them aside without looking up.

'I saw the twins earlier on.' Harold told her.

'You'd love them if you could see them. They're so bonny now.'

Still she didn't react. As he stared round at the other blank faces, he heard a muted scream from a nearby ward. It unleashed a pent up fury in him. Grabbing Edna by the hand, slow and unresponsive with her pudding basin hair cut, he shouted

'You're coming with me. We're getting out of here!'

Chatting nurses looked up astonished. Marching to the end of the room, he demanded to know the procedure for the removal of a voluntary patient. A doctor angrily explained

'But Mr Hunt, your wife's not ready for discharge yet. Not only has she not improved in her two years here, she's shown a severe deterioration!'

'Not a good recommendation!' snapped Harold, slamming the heavy door as he rushed Edna out.

Speeding past autumn woods and haystacked fields, Edna could hardly believe in her freedom. They were half way home before she found the voice to ask

'Are you really taking me away from there Harold? Don't ever send me back again, will you?'

'No I won't Lass,' he answered 'they did you no good in there. Nothing to do but stare at the walls, I'd go crazy there myself in a week! You'll soon get well if you've got something to do, playing bridge, making dresses for the twins.'

He sounded more convinced than he felt, but was determined she shouldn't go back.

As they turned into Windsor Drive, Edna struggled to keep back her tears. She succeeded, afraid for so long to show reactions that could be termed insane. It all seemed unreal, the warm hallway, the bright dining room fire. Places were set for all the family and from the kitchen came appetising odours. The grandmother and two strangely tall daughters hugged and kissed Edna. Then they brought in her favourite tea. There it was, poached salmon and cucumber with new potatoes, fruit scones and a coffee cake.

'When are the babies coming home?' Edna asked.
'Tomorrow Love.' Harold told her.
On their arrival next day, Edna greeted the twins
'Come here little loves!', reaching out for them.
They shrank away, clinging to the skirts of their foster mother. Their own mother was a stranger to them now. Their cries filled the house as Mrs Chapel left, until new toys caught their attention.

Edna's old friend Lilian called round and they took a tram into town. They bought patterns and materials to make dresses for the twins. Also chosen were a crochet needle and salmon pink silky thread, for yet more diminutive outfits. Lilian bought balls of the same thread in blue. Later, Osbert took a snapshot of her son Danny and the twins in their silky outfits, all in a huge rattan basket.

Harold and Edna made up a foursome with the Grants, Lilian and her husband, for a night at the Conservative club. Lulu and Osbert were rushing out too.

'I'm first for the bathroom!' shouted Osbert. |
'No you're not!' said Lulu, 'I'm meeting Larry at seven.'
'Larry the Great!' mocked Osbert, 'O.K. then, but I'm first tomorrow.'

'Now for a bit of peace.' her grandmother said to Bonnie, when the revellers had gone.

'They rush about like geese nicked in the head! It gives me palpitations of the heart.' Bonnie now ten, piled cushions behind her, on one end of the large settee. Her bobbed head scanned a book. Looking up, she said

'Thank goodness those babies are in bed. Things have never been the same since they arrived! Because of them, I had to leave Waverly and go to this horrid council school.'

'Well work hard Love.' her grandmother counselled, 'Pass the scholarship and you'll go to the High School.'

She tried to make Bonnie feel special. For parents' nights out she had thought up a treat. Sitting beside Bonnie, she opened her work box, got out a large tin of toffees and switched on the radio.

'Don't forget, this is our secret!' she smiled.

Heads turned in Thorndale Park, as Lulu and Bonnie pushed the large twin pram. The Edwardian park, facing stone villas, had a war memorial - the Cenotaph. Built on a rise, it was enticingly hidden by tree lined terraces. Stairways were bordered by sweet scented shrubs. At intervals on balustraded walls were flower filled urns. Rising from the monument's semi-circle of columns was a large gilt cross with three roundels. Here, an incident became an enduring memory for Cathy. Deflected light from the cross struck her eye, with a flash of terrifying brilliance. For years she was afraid to glance there, though it could be seen from every angle of the park.

Lilian Grant's home was one of the imposing villas fronting the park. Its bead fringed hall led to rooms flowing with art nouveau curves. Edna envied the Tiffany style lamps, her flare for decor being balked by Harold's outdated views. Lilian was large and flamboyant, her hennaed hair showing grey at the roots, as she rushed from one unfinished plan to another.

'I'd love to make cakes like you do Lilian.' said Edna.

'Well come on, let's try!' encouraged Lilian.

'I'd need great muscular arms like yours.' Edna laughed. She tried, but the creaming of butter and sugar was beyond her. Icing cakes was her forte. She piped rosettes, ribbons and lovely lettering. Her marzipan fruits rivalled those in their favourite cafes.

When Edna took the twins to tea at Lilian's, Danny ran up to them kicking a ball.

'Come on little twins, d' you want to play football?' he invited.

Ignoring him Cathy asked 'Shall we have tea now?' He brought toys and books, but they looked on impassively, until Edna read them all a story. For tea were crustless sandwiches, with scones and fairy cakes to follow.

'Shall we go home now?' asked Cora when they'd eaten, ignoring the crestfallen Danny, bringing more toys. The Hunt twins lived in a world of their own, speaking mostly to each other. Once, sitting on the stairs, Bonnie heard them whispering

'Give it to Percy, he eats gas.'

Then she remembered her father, peering at the kitchen stove and saying

'This thing eats gas, we should go electric.'

At age four, they went to their first Masonic Christmas party, appearing in a sketch of 'Cinderella' Cora and Cathy were two of the fairies in the transformation scene. Edna had toiled eagerly, on white dresses with tutu style skirts. Here and there a rosebud echoed those on their white satin slippers. Each was to carry a silver wand. That morning they visited the hairdressers, their hair transposed into Shirley Temple curls. At four, in blue velvet cloaks, Harold drove them up the Masonic Hall's tree lined drive. Then Edna took them to a make-up session. Chattering mums rouged tender cheeks, enhancing rosebud lips. All went well until the fairies lined up, while the pumpkin turned coach drew across. Edna crimsoned as the twins, upstaging Cinderella, broke ranks. Rushing to the footlights, they swept the stage with their wands!

Edna again began to frequent bridge parties, though she didn't dare hold one herself. She was no great player, but neither were most of the others.

'You'll have to speed up Edna, we're not playing' snap!' sneered a keen member.

'It's not a race either!' shot Edna, voicing her thoughts for once.

The hostesses vied with each other in the spreads they put on. There were minuscule sandwiches, bridge rolls and home made cakes of every kind. It was at one of these parties that Edna met Gloria Swinburne, a teacher of elocution and dance.

'I'd love to have your twins in my classes!' she enthused. 'I'm sure I could bring them out beautifully my dear.'

Edna decided to try it.

Their fringed bobs freshly trimmed, the twins took a tram with their mother to Miss Swinburnes. They approached great gates and saw through passing branches the winking glow of windows, under a snow capped tower. Outwardly they were calm. Fear ebbed as they drew closer. Luxurious plants in a lamp lit conservatory awoke a stirring of interest. A first feeling that there might be pleasure in the unknown......

Facing a gilt framed mirror in the ballroom, their cloned reflection brought back reality. They approached the group of girls, chatting in socially superior tones, while a lone small boy joined in. Having struggled into their patent leather slippers, the twins stood awkwardly on the fringe of the crowd. As Edna combed their sleek brown hair, she thought how pretty they looked, with their oval faces and large grey eyes. She slipped away as Miss Gloria Swinburne made her entrance.

Later, Cathy recalled their taste of elocution. All had to repeat after

Miss Swinburne, copying her gestures,

'Please, may I?', No!, Sorry.'

When the twins' turn came, neither was able to utter a sound. After much persuasion the teacher gave up and the rest of the class declaimed. A solo dance drama followed, by Charles Swinburne Platt, Miss Swinburne's five year old son.   On the way home, Edna asked

'Was it fun then?', Cathy and Cora answered

'No,' refusing to comment any further.

Gradually, shamefaced, Cathy told of their non performance,

'We just couldn't say what the lady wanted.' At Edna's suggestion of their leaving, Harold blew up.

'I've forked out for fees and God knows what else!' he thundered, 'They'll have to carry on!'

The embarrassment of returning was too much for Edna. This time she had her way, but she knew an opportunity had been lost.....

Harold's plumbing business was less than booming. The twins were to go to the local primary, unlike their privately educated siblings. Lacking friends, they continued to revolve around each other. As their fifth birthday neared, Edna told the cloned pair they would start school at Easter. On the day, the sun broke through after rain, gleaming on puddles and wind blown trees. Edna and the children called first at the cemetery to put flowers on their grandfather's grave. Cora stared at a strange bright figure, declaiming before a Catholic crowd.

Inside the door marked infants, a great din of crying loudened.

'What are they crying for Mummy?' asked Cathy.

'Yes, why?' echoed Cora, as Edna prepared to leave.

'Well all the mothers have got to go now and they'll be on their own.' she answered.

'You're lucky you see, you've got each other.

At the sight of slates and chalk, the sisters settled eagerly. The crying gradually ceased as a singing of nursery rhymes got going. The kind teacher, the wall painted ducks, the sight of new activities sprung the twins from their usual apathy.

They loved drawing more and more as they grew. They copied the flowing locks of the Art Nouveau style, featured in Lulu's old books. A page in one of these terrified Cora. She couldn't confess it even to Cathy. Titled 'The Little Men of Crumpletown', a poem was entwined with crooked houses, and their ancient inhabitants. Their faces, wrinkled as Autumn leaves, were redolent of Chinese ivories. Cathy was curious, when her sister quickly turned the page.

On summer afternoons in Thorndale Park, while their parents rested on a seat, the twins would run to a special slope off the main pathways. Here they played their favourite game of 'Sea King's Palace'. In dual imagination they swam under waters of sunlit green, with mermen, mermaids and water babies.

Edna, tiring of the daily journeys, arranged for thirteen-year olds to take her twins to school. The girls laughed, joked and had conversations, often about realities quite alien to the twins. When one spoke of her sister breast feeding her new baby, Cora piped up,

'I don't believe it!'

The girl retorted

'Your mother would have fed you too.'

As if to prove the point she unbuttoned her dress and took out a breast, startling the pair out of their usual detachment. The girls gave the twins donkey rides, to speed up the journey. Hearing of it, the headmistress summoned the twins to her awesome presence. A religious woman, she forbade more rides.

'If you don't use your legs, God will take them away!' she threatened.

It was what the pair wanted. They'd hated the rides, terrified the giggling girls would trip. When asthma slowed them down, Cora pondered on Providential punishment.

Harold was a member of two council committees. The Watch Committee viewed cinemas and theatres, especially the Palace, with its double entendres. The other committee, the Public Assistance, gave second hand clothes and 'Boots for the Bairns', a tiny version of those painted by Lowry. Harold kept a sharp eye open for abuse. He told Edna of a woman with eleven children, all living in one room.

'You know Edna,' he went on, 'We gave her an end terrace and what did she do? We found her in one room again, but making a packet from subletting the rest!'

At school, the older children made Christmas presents for hardship families. Boys carved and painted wooden vehicles, while girls made clothes for small dolls. Before being given to the families, these toys were shown to the whole school. Cathy, toys though she had in plenty, had a guilty longing for one of these dolls. With their porcelain faces and natural hair, each one was attractively boxed. Cathy hoped to get one at the Christmas party, coming up.

The twins begged to wear their last year's white ballet dresses at the party. The most memorable event there was a scramble. The class teacher threw a rubber sheet on the floor, then emptied huge bottles of sweets on the top. At a word the whole class swooped on the pile, grabbing as many as they could hold. The twins shrank back, as shoes and boots went flying. A few sweets weren't worth torn dresses. Their feasts consumed, excitedly screaming, the others went back for more. Then, to the twins' surprise, their teacher beckoned them into a small side room. There on its mat was their own small scramble!

Another Christmas party now looming was the annual Masonic one. For this Edna was speedily finishing dresses. In palest pink net, plain and frilled, they also featured the new puffed sleeves. Cloaked and slippered, the pampered pair tremulously approached the Masonic hall. Chinese lanterns glowed on the lace like branches of its trees. Excitement swept over them as they mounted the lamp lit steps. A heavy scent wafted from a side room, with laughter and clinking of bottle and glass. They gazed at black suited men, chatting with women in georgette or satin. Beyond the swirling cigarette smoke, a children's' game had begun.

Spotting her friend Lilian with her son, Edna and her twins sat beside them.
'Come on Twins!' smiled Danny, ushering them into the games. In musical chairs, Cathy won the prize, a lovely little doll! With Danny they

talked to the other children, who laughed and joked with such ease. After a tea on a great white cloth, Father Christmas arrived on his sledge. Clutching presents, it was home for the twins, as their siblings arrived for the dance. Osbert looked good in white tie and tails. Lulu and Bonnie wore flared creations, by local dressmaker Miss Broom.

The twins said little, their excitement now faded, as their grandmother put them to bed. Harold and Edna returned to the dance, but only on Harold's terms – no cocktails for Edna. Usually teetotal himself, he was afraid that drink might release an embarrassing Edna, wild and unpredictable........ He kept a careful eye on Lulu, though frugal Larry wouldn't buy over much.

'Larry' she whispered, stroking his dark wavy hair, 'I love you but you could be more generous.'

Later, she would sneak up to bed with a mouthful of mints, in case of parental confrontation. Blond Osbert's film star looks were much in demand, but he kept an eye on Bonnie and her partners. Though irked by Harold's dictatorial ways, Edna's expression was as usual bland. As those around her began to laugh at less than witty remarks, she looked back on an enjoyable if sober evening.

Chapter 3

As Edna sat knitting on a curvaceous park seat, the twins wandered along fragrant sunlit paths.

'It's such a lovely day Mummy! Can we wear our pink party dresses in the park?' they had asked and now they had them on.

They approached a gateway previously unknown, opening onto an old stone terrace. A small boy and three girls came in, arm in arm, laughing and chatting. Clothed almost in rags, they stopped and gasped at the double vision in frilly pink net.

'Ooo!', they breathed as they gazed.

The twins stared coolly, side by side but not close. Their grey eyes lowered as they passed the group.

Next September the twins were kept back in the same class, as their 'three Rs' were coming on slowly. Art and crafts were their forte. In an art session, Cathy was thrilled with her sun bright daisy, its rolled green stem free of white paste.

Cora's embroided square was very neat, its stitches small.

Another girl asked to borrow it and Cora agreed. Cathy was angry, 'You should never have given it to her. She'll say it's hers.'

The girl's mother, one of Edna's bridge friends, showed the work around as being her daughter's. Edna, furious, countered the woman's claim and got back the sample, keeping it in a drawer for years.

'Stick to your guns Cora!' she advised, knowing how hard it was to stick up to Harold.

During the interminable school prayers, several children each term would flutter down in a faint. A new teacher set a precedent by being the first of the staff to succumb. Crying out, glasses flying, all six foot of him crashed to the floor. Children scattered. Cora was almost crushed as she reached for his glasses.

Aged seven, the twins collected film star cigarette cards, filling their little red albums. Eyes alight, they swopped such names as Lorreta Young,

Ronald Coleman and Erroll Flynn. Osbert would hand them a few, puffing on a cigarette as he dashed from the house. Harold gave them cards from his boxes of a hundred, always open on the sideboard. The twins' coughs echoed through the smoky rooms. At school, Mae West was the rage. The girls there mouthed her

'Come up and see me sometime......', their child bodies swaying seductively.

Forbidden the cinema, the twins never saw the stars until years later on their TV screens. On the council watch committee, Harold and his colleagues continued to watch suspect films.

'Edna,' he cried one lunch time, 'George Armitage has burst a blood vessel, watching a Mae West film!'

Banned not only from films but from radio's Children's Hour, the twins felt more and more alienated at school, especially Cathy. While Cora enjoyed Enid Blyton, Cathy favoured books about dream worlds, particularly one, in which terrestrial colours turned into their opposites. A sun of brilliant pink, rose in a saffron sky, over red-purple trees.......

The Windsor Drive sweet shop, near the more opulent New South Road, was often patronised by uniformed girls from Waverley private school. While Cathy and Cora were buying a halfpenny sweet, these girls would come in and ask

'Have you a penny packet of peppermints?'

Their clipped tones cut sharply through other customers' speech. Trying on toy rings from their halfpenny turnovers, the twins couldn't believe that Lulu and Bonnie had once been Waverly pupils.

In the vicinity was Leighton Fields, a favourite route to and from Springfield School. On hot days the twins would wander home that way, sensing enchantment there. Skirting tall grasses, high walls shaded the oriel windows and great conservatory of a Gothic style mansion. Nearby a slightly lower wall revealed the simpler lines of the neo Georgian. Further along, trees around a pseudo castle, shimmered in the bright sun.

The first of these miniature palaces faced onto New South Road. This road ran from the town centre in the direction of similar woollen towns.

A far vista of turrets and cupolas, rising from surrounding trees, carried on to distant blue. When told in school prayers of the heavenly mansions, the twins envisioned these half glimpsed towers.

The Hunt family disapproved of their youngsters going home through Leighton Fields, as it was so lonely. One evening their curiosity got the better of the twins and they ventured up one of the mysterious tree lined drives. Bushes gave way to a lawn and flower beds.
'Look, tulips, daffodils!'
'Still a few crocuses!' Cora and Cathy took in the scene.
Reluctantly they drifted back behind trees. Soon after, a macintoshed man stepped out of the bushes revealing his 'glory'. Startled but innocently unafraid, the pair ran off, giggling as they neared Windsor Drive. At home Cora began
'Mummy we saw something weird in a garden.....'
Harold's face darkened as they carried on.
'Never go that way again!' he thundered 'Or you'll get the strap!'
'The strap', an old leather belt, hung on a nail in the kitchen. Though never used, its threat was enough to scare the twins. Reluctantly they gave up their evening wanderings.

'Eh Edna, I'd give threepence if I were washed!' quipped Grandma, struggling out of her bed. On cold mornings Cathy and Cora got dressed by her bedroom fire. As they dived into liberty bodices, Edna dressed Grandma in her antiquated underwear, made at Miss Broom's in the style of Gran's youth. These were a red flannel chemise and a pair of striped 'drawers', so called because of their draw-string waists.
'Like something from Blackpool Tower Circus.' Lulu said. Edna had tried to update Gran's underwear, but she refused even Directoire knickers. She still used a wash bowl with a matching jug. Filled by Edna who washed her each morning, the bowl stood on the walnut dressing table. It matched the wardrobe and an enormous bed, part of a job lot acquired by their grandfather.

On this particular day, Edna planned a visit to Miss Broom's, to give her an important order. Lulu was to have a June marriage. She would choose styles for her honeymoon and wedding. Miss Broom's tiny front room with sewing machine, patterns and fresh new materials, held a special excitement that day. Lulu chose white crepe de chine, to wear with her grandmother's veil. The bridesmaids would also wear crepe de chine in pastel shades of blue green and lemon. They chose frilled dresses, the fashion that year, but with Victorian posies and bonnets. There was much travelling to and from fittings before Lulu's great day arrived.

That Christmas was remembered by Cathy for not going to the school party. Cora had had chicken pox and was over it, when Cathy discovered a spot. She attempted to hide it but soon there were more. Half afraid of the socially embarrassing party, she was more disappointed at missing her present. Delight greeted Cora's return with two parcels. Cathy's contained a basket work table and chairs, miniatures of those which graced the new Ritz cinema cafe.

Unfortunately the twins got head lice that Christmas and went back to school with a concoction on their hair.

'Something in this room is making me feel quite sick!' announced the teacher.

'Will whoever's responsible please stand up' The twins sheepishly stood up and confessed, to the accompaniment of jeers from the class, especially loud from the matted haired Thorpe twins whose nits were permanent. Edna's heroic combing and squashing of the beasts onto newspaper soon got rid of the horror.

Later in their cloakroom, the girls took off all but vests and navy blue knickers, for drill. More fortunate girls whispered

'Look at that kilt!', as one child took off her jumper to reveal a kilt top in need of a wash.

The girl shouted back,

'Mucky kilts are t' best!' Headed by the Thorpe twins, others without the benefits of home hot water joined in.

'Mucky kilts, mucky kilts are t' best!', they sang and danced until angry staff ended the show.

Cathy and Cora now suffered continuously from asthma, their wheezing an embarrassment to themselves and others. On their doctor's advice, each morning, Edna would slap on their chests a piece of lint smeared with a heated concoction known as antiphlogistine. Painfully hot on contact, as it cooled it would break up and drop through their clothes, to the derisive hoots of their classmates.

'What 'ave them twins got on now?' they would smirk.

Recalling the substance years later, Cathy realised it was named after Phlogiston, an imaginary element forgotten for two centuries.

11 Windsor Drive was in pre wedding fever, when a minor catastrophe struck.

'I love this dress.' Lulu murmured while ironing. 'It reminds me of the night that Larry and I met.....'

'Starry skies and all that.' smiled Bonnie, but some stars disappeared from the star spattered creation, reappearing on the base of the iron!

The dress in midnight blue was the highlight of the collection.

'I've nothing to wear now for dinner and dancing!' sobbed Lulu, until Bonnie went hunting for a midnight blue rose.

On the wedding morning, a capacity crowd filled the house. Larry's sleek auburn haired brother, already in morning suit, popped up to the attic to wake hung-over Osbert. He smiled at the small double image on the stairs. The twins had on only their 'opera top' vests, scarcely covering their navels. At the sight of him they rushed back into their room in embarrasment, a feeling that returned on later meetings.

Grandma sat from eight in the morning in her toque and veil, stick by her side, watching the wedding preparations. Severe under the tight veil, not a cup of tea passed her lips until the reception.

'This bonnet looks hideous!' exclaimed Bonnie, glancing in the mantelpiece mirror.

Its pale green pleats, rising above her wavy blond hair, emphasised the long chin, so like her mother's. She certainly looked prettier than Larry's sister Sarah in blue. Tall and buck toothed, she was used to her looks and seemed unconcerned.

The wedding was quiet and all went off beautifully. Under a bright sun,

a photographer took shots for a black and white album. The only tense moment was after the reception at the George, Huddersfield's poshest hotel. Larry's brother Tony on leave from the Gold Coast, spied a black man standing at the bar. He immediately announced in his Oxford tones,
'I'm not drinking with that!'
Though Edna mildly protested, she was ignored. The wedding party trooped, sheep-like, to the nearby Queen's Hotel.

Much envied by Bonnie and the twins in her pale pink going away suit, with pink fox fur collar and diminutive hat, Lulu joined Larry in his blue two-seater. It was rattling with old shoes and plumbing spares put there by Osbert. After a duly rapturous honeymoon, the couple moved into their semi-detached home. A year later, almost to the day, Peter Hunt Dennison was born. Cathy and Cora, at eight, were thrilled to become aunts, though no one believed them at school.

'No love, it'll be your cousin' was the usual retort.

They dutifully knitted small woollen garments, but, as the centre of attention in the family shifted from them to the new arrival, their fierce jealousy surprised them.

Larry, a garden enthusiast when not playing cricket, filled his front borders with colourful plants. In the back, behind sweet-pea trellises, he made a kitchen garden. The house, at the end of a cul-de-sac, backed onto woodland. In spring and summer the visiting twins would sit in the garden or wander in what to them was a forest. Aware in this home of a sensuous warmth outside their experience, they shrank from their return to the ageing Harold and Edna.

One weekend they were asked to baby-sit, staying the night. As Larry waited at the open door, Lulu scuttled around like an over dressed crab, giving last minute hints,

'You know where the biscuits are. Make yourselves a drink.'

Settling down to a radio play, it was half over when Peter began crying. Pulling back his covers, the twins stared at the wet nappy's enormous pin.

'I'll change him, if you hold him down.' Cath said dubiously, pulling

down the cot side.
'It looks a bit slack.' said Cora of the clean nappy.
'Leave it, I'll prick him if I do it again.' Cathy snapped.
The nappy was kicked off, the bed wet through!
'Inefficiency Personified' Larry christened the pair.

For several evenings, sitting cosily by the fire, Edna was absorbed by a book. She had almost finished it when Harold, thinking it was one of her usual novels, noticed the title, 'All About Freemasonry'

'What do you think you're playing at?' he bawled, snatching the book from her hand, 'You know members of the society are sworn to secrecy!'

Flicking through a few pages, he then threw it onto the blazing coals. This was the first, though not the last, of his book burning. Having secretly read the book earlier, Edna didn't worry. She merely said

'That cost half a crown!'

'And whose half-crown was it?' returned Harold. Roaring at the entire family

'Don't dare to read anything that I disapprove of!' he flounced out to his Masonic Lodge.

Since rescuing his wife from the mental hospital, Harold's earlier kind forbearance was less in evidence. Though Edna now had an account at the town's plushest department store, she seldom used it. A recent exception was the purchase of a lace evening gown in deep red with a matching stole. In it she felt like Margaret Dumont in 'A Night at the Opera', mature but still attractive. Wearing it for a Masonic ladies' evening, it didn't take Harold long to destroy her illusion.

'You look like a jar of Robertson's jam without the golly' he commented.

'I'll be taking the golly with me' she thought, mindful of his Masonic regalia.

She determined that he wouldn't spoil her evening.

The car pulled up as they neared the twin lamps of the Masonic hall. Lilian and friends thought the dress lovely, its stole swirling as they entered from the chilly night air. Lilian's dress was patterned in russets and golds. With her hennaed hair she looked magnificent. The dress, her own creation, had faults but Edna would never comment. Unlike Mrs Collingwood, passing at that moment. Flicking at the skirt of Lilian's dress she remarked

'Artificial of course but very pretty.'

As they passed the bar, a richness of wines and cigars put them in party mood. Finding their places at dinner, white cloths and silver service gleamed against colourful dresses. Masonic aprons added brilliance. The food surpassed expectations Tempting dishes led to the main course. The bronzed skin of fresh roasted turkey nestled among sprouts and duchesse potatoes, with forcemeat balls stuffing and cranberry sauce. Queen's pudding followed then coffee and mints. After the meal they joined foxtrotting friends.

After a school clinic visit, Cathy and Cora brought home an envelope. Edna was shocked to read that the two of them were suffering from malnutrition. Her first thought was what on earth Harold would say. For years she had tried to coax them into finishing meals, but with little success. When she took them out they would eat lots and ask for more. She felt people thought them half starved. Lulu didn't help with her constant carping,

'You'll never get nice young men! Look at your knobbly knees!'

Lunch over, Edna geared herself up to give Harold the envelope, but he seemed keen to recall his day. Canvassing for renewal of his seat on the council, he had entered a courtyard and watched a small boy. Alone, in charity boots and old clothes, he danced and sang as he ate from a bag.

'I'mh'avin' a pennoth of chats, I'm havin' a pennoth of chats.'

Products of fish and chip shops, the chats were made from new potatoes too small to be chipped. Harold had tiptoed away not wishing to disturb. He then turned to areas more likely to vote conservative. In memory, he compared the eagerness of the child to the lacklustre gaze of his pampered twins. To Edna's surprise, he didn't seem bothered by the letter.

Diphtheria swept Huddersfield that Summer. Harold had decreed that the twins be kept from the park paddling pool, in case of infection. Cora pestered

'Please can we go in the pool, it's so hot?'
'Every one else does.' complained Cathy.

So one hot day Edna took them to the pool. Next day Cathy had an extremely sore throat. Diagnosed as a carrier of diphtheria, she was swiftly sent off to hospital. Edna had resorted to Grandma's suggestion of a poultice, to ease Cathy's throat. Soaked in some ancient concoction, it was fastened with a large safety pin.

'What in heaven's name is this?' laughed the nurses, roughly ripping off the poultice.

Cold hands chilled the feverish child as they put on a starchy nightdress. Thinking of her mother, Cathy shed a few tears when the lovingly placed poultice was gone.

Cathy's bed was at one end of a ward. She listened to other children's laughter and talk but was too far away to join in. Scarcely speaking through the lonely two months, only her drawing and rereading of books kept her sane. Other children's parents came weekly and talked to them outside the tall windows. They brought fruit to be left at their bedsides Cathy asked why her parents never came or brought fruit.

'Your father has fruit sent for the whole ward my dear.' replied Sister, but Cathy felt no less neglected.

Two months later, she sat outside the ward wrapped in blankets, looking over the kitchen garden.

'You're going home today!' a nurse told her, bringing her unremembered dress. Ramming it on, the woman fastened it back to front. The Hunts arrived at last to pick up their child. Seeing her expressionless, in a back to front frock, Harold finally realised that something was wrong. He began a refrain he would repeat down the years.

'We'll have to watch that one, she's too much like her mother!'

Remembering the hospital questions that Edna couldn't answer, he would dredge up some mental arithmetic for Cathy. Pressurised, she could never get it right, though Cora could.

Bonnie at seventeen had embarked on a secretarial course. Now man-mad, in order to impress at the new Ritz ballroom, she had bought dresses on Edna's little used account. Harold found out.

'I'll be bankrupt before you've finished!' he ranted.

'I'm leaving this minute!' Bonnie retaliated. The grandmother cried

'It's like Bedlam in here!' and went straight to bed. As things calmed down, Harold paid up and Bonnie saved up.

Passing Jesse Lumbs, a local mill, when out with his twins, Harold warned

'If you don't pass the scholarship – it's Jesse Lumbs!' Though they knew he was joking, it spurred the pair on.

At ten they moved to the class of Gerard Beaumont, who specialised in eleven plus training. Beaumont could be cruel. When a chalk faced child asked

'Please Sir can I cross the yard?', he snapped

'If you want to vomit lad, sey so and get out!'

He could be considerate at times. After asking the class to name a beautiful object, one excited reply was

'A new painted double decker bus Sir!' Expecting sarcasm, his kind explanation of current views surprised the class.

About this time, inspectors arrived and gave the class a 'draw a man' test. This was part of a series designed by Cyril Burt, to pick out children of special ability. A psychologist, he was intent on proving the truth of his theories on inherited intelligence, by hook or, as it later appeared, by crook. Paper and pencils on desks, a time was set for the drawing of a man. As work progressed Beaumont and the two inspectors strolled round. When the trio reached Cora, an inspector exclaimed

'The child's an artist!'

He looked down at the miniature man, his face in three quarter view, his limbs naturally placed. As Beaumont explained that Cora had a twin, the three rushed over to Cathy remarking

'The other's the same!'

The anti climax stayed with Cathy. Though realistically detailed, the twins' drawings lacked the immediacy of most children's work. From then on however, they were bent on being artists, naively unaware of the problems ahead.

Cathy had never caught up in arithmetic since her two months in hospital at eight. Unfortunately, after taking the eleven plus in intelligence and English, she was rushed into hospital again, this time with scarlet fever. She missed the arithmetic test. Meanwhile Cora, though missing her sister, was enjoying the extra attention. When Cathy was well, Harold put wheels into motion. The education committee arranged a test for Cathy alone, but she failed again.

'Well the silly bugger!' laughed Harold, at a wedding photo in the Huddersfield Examiner.

It was of the twins' headmaster, a bald elderly widower. He was here complete with a young attractive bride, plus a head of wavy grey hair. Jokes and sniggers followed him around but he persevered with his wig until it was too familiar for comment. Furious at Cathy's failure in maths, Harold organised another re-sit, with the headmaster in attendance this time. Unfortunately she failed yet again. In the end Cathy did get to grammar school.

'My Dad won't let me go to that school.' said a classmate,

'I've got to work in t' mill when I'm fourteen. He said what do I want to go there for? Apin' my betters!'

Others with only two passes, like Cathy, took up the vacancies on offer.

That summer the family gave another order to Miss Broom, for the regulation school blouses and tunics. When they arrived, the twins opened the parcel, with its fresh smell of new fabric. They tried them on, looking at each other to see the effect, no mirror needed. By the time they had bought all the items on the list, Harold erupted.

'No wonder poor buggers can't afford these schools. It's nearly bankrupted me!'

For the last time in their old playground, the twins stood, dual loners, watching the communal skipping. To shouts of 'Pepper, Pepper!' the rope

swirled faster and faster and some dropped out. The cries of
'Nebuchadnezzer, the King of the Jews, bought his wife a pair of shoes......' swamped all other sounds.

Chapter 4

'Twas on the Isle of Capri that I found her,' sang Bonnie, as she ironed her two-tone camiknickers in air force blue and dusty pink. Cathy looked enviously at the gleaming curves, aware of her own body, at twelve, flat chested as a boy's. Bonnie's fiance was Cyril Anthony Jocelyn Joyce, a great favourite with the twins. Fresh face confidently smiling, his clothes were kept immaculate by his doting mother. Through him the twins found their enduring delight, 'Arthur Mee's Childrens Encyclopaedia'. They now spent most Saturdays at his home. While the lovers escaped from the mother's possessive eye, the twins, deep in the library's leather armchairs, would leaf through the Victorian edition. They became so addicted that Harold bought them an updated version for Christmas.

Edna feared that this out-of-school book work would hamper the twins' social performance.

'You know Harold' she mused, 'I'm sorry I stopped the twins' going to Miss Swinburne's. I think they should go to a ballroom class now.'

'As long as it doesn't waste a fortune like last time' said Harold, 'I said then you should have let them carry on.'

Thankful to avoid a row, Edna arranged lessons in ballroom and tap. With Cathy in the lead, the twins circled clumsily to Victor Sylvester's metronome beat. Their favourite dance was a slow Gavotte to the old piano. In a romanticised past they felt more at ease. Later in a local milk bar, her mouth frothy with strawberry milk shake, Cathy felt she was one of the girls.

The twins joined a club run by one of the class. They filled in grubby forms and tried joining in the chatter, but they still felt apart. First Cora and then Cathy gave it up. They returned to their peering at encyclopaedias. When dancing classes finished at Easter, they reverted to their binary existence.

Bonnie and Cyril booked a holiday in Spain, but the Civil War intervened. They had scarcely disembarked, when the travel firm cancelled the tour. On her return, Bonnie had developed extreme left views. These were anathema to Harold, whose solid conservatism suggested action. The Left Book Club's little red books tumbled into the letter box, usually with the very first post. Bonnie crept down each morning. If she saw one she hid it away. If Harold got there first, he consigned yet another to the dining room fire.

'What would Tory councillors think of this rubbish coming here!' he roared.

Bonnie murmured 'Has he never heard of freedom of thought.....'

In secret, she poured over the books, covering every form of socialism. Only National Socialism was absent!

Much influenced by reading about free love, Bonnie broke off her engagement to Cyril. Harold feared she would put these ideas into practice. Another reason for the break was Cyril's desire for children. The arrival of the screaming twins, and their mother being snatched away, had killed any such longing on Bonnie's part. She craved for love and affection from men, but when the talk drifted to domesticity, she would rush on to the next affair. In whatever was new, her blond hair ravishingly set, she would saunter out nightly with her unattractive friend as foil. Whistles followed Shirley's auburn perm, her high fashion on five inch heels. They recoiled when, turning, she revealed the signs of her congenital disease, flattened features and nose hollowed at the bridge. The careful make up concealed nothing.

'You're getting to be a byword in the town!' Harold raged, but Bonnie was unimpressed.

As the war against Hitler had begun, school entry had been put back for some monhs, so that it was January before the Hunt twins started at Thorndale High School for Girls. The great hall was pungent with moth-balls, to those near Miss Withers, the rotund headmistress. She ended prayers with welcoming words for the newcomers. The day rushed by like a speeded-up film to the twins, in separate classes now, more for the benefit of staff than for theirs. They were herded into different rooms for each subject, to their own utter bewilderment.

Their homeward journey led through Thorndale Park, once the grounds of the old hall that was now their school. As the sky darkened, Cathy and Cora struggled through deepening snow, their faces slashed by unseen branches until Cora cried

'There are the gateposts!'

Gasping with relief, they ran between the gateless posts and hurried home.

Warming their hands at the hall radiator, the excruciating pain brought the pair near to tears. Flinging off their coats, they entered the dining-living room to be greeted by Harold.

'What do you think of this girls, the new war bread?' he asked.

Their eyes fell on the white clothed table, set but almost empty. At its centre was an uncut loaf as full of holes as a gruyere cheese. It was too much. Tears streamed down their new uniforms.

'Nay Lasses, it were just a joke!' smiled Grandma, as Bonnie and Osbert stifled their mirth.

It took some time to console the girls, when they saw they'd been fooled. The nauseous object was merely a sponge!

Osbert too was having his problems. For some years he had worked with his father, learning plumbing the hard way. As he climbed on roofs or grovelled in manholes, he loathed the job more each day. He expected his call-up any time, but doubted he would pass. An ankle injury at tennis would mean a C3 at best, he hoped. Apart from work, he avoided his father whenever possible. The sight of Harold's face intensified his stutter, with its heavy eyebrows and readiness for sarcasm. Guilt added to his fear. Harold had put him on a sanitary engineering course. Having missed some classes at the start, he couldn't cope. As a result, he had stopped going altogether, spending the time at cinemas or pubs with friends. He knew his father would find out and dreaded the resulting explosion. His heart began pounding when Harold announced

'I'd like a few words in the drawing room Lad.'

Already Harold had lost employees to the forces. He was thinking of closing down the business for the 'duration'. He had hoped that Osbert would show some spirit and volunteer. Alternately, he felt he must give his son the same chance of a let out as his own father had provided in the previous war. Harold had been in the Territorials, when his father by means of his masonic connections, had offered him a reserved occupation. He had accepted, but with a shame that still lingered. He hoped that his son would refuse the offer, though he knew it was unlikely.

'Sit down lad, I've something to tell you' he said, as he led the way to the warm drawing room.

The pre-heating of the room was so unusual that Osbert felt still more uneasy. His fears subsided as Harold spelled out his offer. Osbert accepted and Harold made the arrangements, though disappointed. Within weeks Osbert was working as a lead burner with an odd collection of misfits. One even came dressed for the office, ashamed to be seen in overalls in the streets.

The twins had begun to irritate Miss Dartery, known as 'the Dart' Her subjects were music and scripture. Unmarried, having lost her fiancee at Passchendaele, she was nearing retirement. Still slim, traces of youthful attraction were now and then apparent. She was well liked by the girls – loved even, by a select band. These spent weekends at her home. For them she used her not inconsiderable influence in musical circles.

'Call me Dart' she would say to this favoured group.

Cathy and Cora were not among the chosen. The teacher felt a decided antipathy towards Cathy, seeing the child's cold detachment as inhuman. During one scripture lesson, Miss Dartery asked the question

'What is your idea of Hell?'

Several hands shot up and their owners gave lengthy answers. Cathy raised her arm to ask

'Could Hell be life on Earth Miss Dartery?'

Before speaking three words she was cut short by the remark,

'You don't believe in Hell! Sit down!'

Music lessons were also a trial to the twins. They were technically at sea, never having learnt the piano. However, Miss Dart's recordings had sown spores that would later mushroom. Mozart's Cherubino's love song fell like a brilliant rain on the desert of their emotional lives. Unhappily, instead of a recording, the mistress herself sang an aria from the opera. This provoked laughter, quickly suppressed. Unfortunately for Cathy, in her open mouthed astonishment at their rudeness, the Dart saw mockery. She banished both twins from the choir.

'Don't let me see either of you here again' she thundered.

'I still remember your sister Bonnie and all the trouble she caused!'

A classmate, sorry for the twins, invited them to join her Guide company. Though feeling apart from the other Guides, whose private jokes they could never fathom, the twins' uniforms gave them some sense of belonging. They enthusiastically began to compete for badges. Visits to a creche in a seedy part of town, to gain Child Nurse badges, almost ended their Guiding for good.

As the sky darkened in the unlit street, the twins waited for a home bound bus. To the queue's horror, a girl ran out of a nearby tenement, pursued by a khaki clad figure. The American raped her in front of the crowd. In their state of shock, a bus passed by unnoticed. Cora, innocent of the event's significance, put out her hand and stopped the next one. The twins remembered the threats they'd had when they told of the mackintoshed flasher. This time discretion prevailed and they kept their mouths shut. Reading a newspaper report of the incident, Harold forbade them the area, so bolting the proverbial door.

Cathy and Cora set off with the Guides on a camping trip to South Yorkshire. As they approached the mining village, the great wheel, stark against brooding clouds, dwarfed blackened cottages. Stunted inhabitants shuffled by in faded garments, little better than rags. The place seemed even more depressing than their own West Riding. As they helped to put up tents in a downpour, the pair were glad they wouldn't be there long. Sun broke through the campfire haze, as hassled guides served breakfast. This was burnt toast and wasp laden marmalade. Cathy exclaimed

'This toast 's burnt!' Cora followed with

'Let the wasps eat it!'

Furious glares made them aware of the unspoken rule of never complaining in wartime. Ordered to clean the dixies as punishment, they spent hours on the job. When Cora's had shed its blackened skin, it shone like sterling silver.

Supervising the laying of trails in the woods, Captain and Lieutenant had forgotten the punishment. They started a hunt for the missing twins. When they found them, polishing their cauldrons like miniature witches, Captain finally exploded.
'How stupidly conscientious!' she stormed, 'You must have heard shouts! We've been scouring the countryside for hours!'
'I'll see you two don't go camping again!' was her final verdict.

Always trailing behind, panting and wheezing, the pair struggled to keep to the schedule. That evening, exhausted, they thankfully flopped on the grass around the campfire. Captain led the girls in cleaned up versions of old army songs. It pelted on Sunday. Drying plates with sopping wet tea towels, they sighted through trees, the bright scarlet bus. A gloom settled at the thought of their homecoming.

At the start of the war, Harold had ignored the warnings against hording. Piled high on the kitchen shelf was a store of Kellogg's Corn Flakes, Ryvita and Canada First beans. These were the foods preferred by his family, especially the pampered twins. Always fussy, the two accepted the wartime food better than expected. Clothing was more of a problem for Bonnie. Despite coupons, with the sewing machine's help, she still turned available heads. With material printed with marigolds, Edna began new dresses for the twins. Trying hers on, Cora complained
'These sleeves are too wide! They make our arms look thinner than ever.'
'When they complain they make their own' Edna said.
So not unwillingly, the twins finished the dresses themselves.

Cora and Cathy were on a Sunday morning stroll. Looking towards the chapel on the brow of the hill, they saw an astonishing sight. Not one but two Miss Withers headed the worshippers leaving the chapel. Though one twin wore black, the other brown, our twins couldn't pick out their own headmistress! They hurried home with their news.

'Guess what we've just seen – double Miss Withers!' Cathy called to Bonnie, still in her dressing gown with a hangover.

'You saw the other half. I'd heard there was one.' Bonnie smiled languidly.

'They're both head teachers you know.' The one in brown's retired,' chimed in Edna, 'Her school's been closed for the duration.'

Some Saturday mornings after shopping, Edna would take the twins to Heal's Cafe. Among potted palms and curlicued hat stands, they ate marzipan fruits and overheard chatter. The talk was of Mary Collingwood's divorce, no surprise. For years rumours had spread that her terror of sex was ruining her marriage. Lilian and Edna were agog at the news.

'Have you heard about the Collingwoods' divorce?' asked Lilian, looking smart in her sporty outfit.

'No wonder Norman went wandering!' Edna added, 'She'll make that son of hers just the same, watching his every move.' Mary Collingwood, just then approaching, bitched

'I love your sporty outfit Lilian. Of course it wouldn't suit me, I'm drawing room!'

Such fragments of overheard talk aroused the twins' curiosity. Afraid to ask about sex, they took to frequenting a certain book shop. Tucked in an alcove, they gained enlightenment from Marie Stopes and others. Some of the advice given to newly weds seemed bizarre.

'Chase your bride round the honeymoon suite.' hardly seemed likely to arouse desire, as suggested.

They came to the shop every Friday, after school.

Eventually, they got over confident. Staff spotted them and rang Windsor Drive. Fortunately it was Edna who picked up the phone. Without mentioning it to Harold, she bought the twins a discreet book for girls. It was mainly diagrams, but they contented themselves with it, thankful to be spared 'the strap'. They learned little of sex at their school, staffed only by unmarried women. The biology mistress volunteered to

teach sex. Her remark
'The male rabbit should never have hot baths' made the girls' day.

At the first hints of war, Harold began building an air raid shelter. Six feet deep in his wild back garden, it had a pump, bunks and a heating system. Topped with concrete, steps led to its hollowed interior. At the sound of the first siren, Harold proudly herded his family down, returning with Osbert for Grandma.

'Nay Harold, don't turn me out of my bed, I'll catch my death of pneumonia!' she cried.

Her unbound hair floated on the night wind like a pathetic ghost.

'You're here and you're stopping here Mother!' insisted Harold, as he lowered her into the torch lit depths.

The shelter however, was of little use. Only one bomb was ever dropped on Huddersfield. It fell harmlessly into a mill dam.

Miss La Farge, French mistress at Thorndale school, wore jewellery and dresses in sophisticated tones. She wore her waving hair loosely in a bun. Her subtle smile suggested she let it down rather more often than other staff members. Tall, slim, she contrasted strangely with the square butch gym mistress who shared her flat. Rumoured to be Lesbians, they had rooms in a remote mansion on the outskirts of the town.

Cathy loved French lessons, enlivened by a wit that was rare in the dreary establishment. Her neurotic handwriting, liberally sprinkled with blots, had caused annoyance to staff. The Headmistress herself had labelled it 'lacking in character.' In one session, Miss La Farge pointed out an apparent mistake. She flushed at Cathy's insistence that an 'a' not an 'o' was intended.

'What confounded cheek!' she commented, 'Be in this room at four o'clock and repeat writing the line 'I will not be impertinent', until I come back.'

Returning at four fifteen she saw a slight figure threading its way down the wide staircase. She began a tirade
'More insolence!', until the sweet mouth told her that this was the other twin, Cora.

Harold had finally given up his business interests for 'the duration' He had felt so ill recently that he thought he would never see peace. His doctor had diagnosed athlete's heart, but he feared that this wasn't all. He spent many evenings at his office, fire watching as he called it, with the family dog. Cyril had bought it for Bonnie, after their abortive holiday in Spain. Harold had adopted it, as she showed little interest. Called Pedro, it was a pedigree wire-haired fox terrier, with an unpronounceable name. Harold was very fond of the dog, and wouldn't hear of it being put down, though it had already bitten his mother. Its woolly head would peer invitingly through a hole in the hedge. When passers by attempted to stroke it, it would snap alarmingly. Police had already issued a warning.

Harold grew thin with hanging flesh, his face the hue of yellowing paint. After one of his walks with Pedro, he sank into his chair by the fire.

'I've just seen old Schofield and what do you think he said?' he faltered to Edna.

'What's the matter with you Harold lad? You're goin' home!'

Edna could think of little in reply. Their doctor had advised her to keep quiet about his cancer, but how long could she keep this up? Tears threatened and she ran upstairs with the excuse that his mother was calling. Now bedridden, the matriarch constantly complained

'Eh Edna, I wish the Lord would take me!', as the diminutive Edna rushed up and down stairs.

The twins' reading habits tended to roam along differing paths, though occasionally they would poach from each other. Cora read books about boarding schools, in common with most of her class. Such books as the new 'Chalet School' series. Angela Brazil's books appealed to Cathy, with their lily leafed covers in subtle greens Then a phrase roused a quick anger. This came in a passage about a music teacher, too good to teach 'shopkeeper's daughters from Warford' As a plumber's daughter from Yorkshire, she felt affronted. Closing the book, she wondered why other girls didn't feel the sting. She turned to her normal escapist fare with relief. The blood drunken Gods of ancient Peru were too distant in time and space to offend.

While in bed with flu, she began reading a children's book, which touched on the views of the atheist Bradlaugh. As she read on, remembered passages from the Children's Encyclopaedias took on new meaning. Far regions of space, where empty planets whirled about distant suns, seemed all there was. No caring God or cosy heaven lay pleasantly in wait. She could only think that Bradlaugh was right.......

A year after their earlier guide camp, Cathy and Cora were about to go camping again. Rangers now, they loved their smart new uniforms, grey sweaters, navy berets and skirts, but wished they could fill them out better. This time around, they could walk to the camp, a mere hundred yards from their home. A winding lane, known as 'the Snicket" ran between Windsor Drive and the campsite. Over the wall tents could be seen. They thought excitedly of lying among scented grass, sighting the stars through treetops. Close to the tents was their Guide hut, the ground being owned by Mrs Fuller, the District Commissioner. Approaching, they glimpsed her home, spire and turrets in delightful asymmetry, with lawns, pathways and green painted seats. Hidden from view, a broadening drive swept to the new south road.

The twins, never completely at ease in camp, withdrew still more at the arrival of the holiday guides. These, mostly Rangers, were at boarding schools during term time Their arrogant manner endlessly proclaimed their superiority. Alison Fuller, daughter of the District Commissioner, had a superior air. There was the glance, starting at the feet of her inferiors and sweeping to the face and beyond, a hint of a sneer on the lips........ Like other mill owners in the eighteen hundreds, the Fullers had heaved themselves out of obscurity, on the backs of those employed in their mills. In as few as two generations of so-called public education, all traces of their forebears had vanished.

Musing vaguely along these lines, Cathy awoke to the present, as Cora showed her a list of sleeping arrangements.
'Look!' she exclaimed, 'We're not sleeping in tents at all, we're being put in the guide hut'
Cathy was livid.

'It's mum, interfering again!' she cried, 'Can't she ever let us behave like other people? Come on, let's go to Captain' Cora disagreed,
'No, don't let's bother, you know how they hate complaining.'
'Well, I'm going anyway!' Cathy determined.

Cora capitulating, they marched off to where Captain and Lieutenant were hoisting the flag. The Guide Captain groaned inwardly as she saw the two approaching. Angry tears almost prevented speech for Cathy.
'What's the matter love, are you homesick?' asked the lieutenant sympathetically. This was too much for Cathy,
'Homesick!' she shouted, the whole camp looking up astonished. She could almost have killed her mother at that moment. Her fury was untempered by affection, as she gave vent to frustration between sobs.
'I could see this was coming.' Captain snapped. 'I told your mother you'd be perfectly allright in the tents. I altered the list and now I suppose I'll have to change it back.', she went on. 'Allright then, I'll put you back in the tents.'

'Peace I ask of thee oh River, Peace Peace Peace.'
Later that evening the Guides' favourite camp fire song, American Indian, rose above drifting smoke. The late sun cast shadowed towers and parapets at their feet. As the weekend finished, Captain remembered that she had promised to weigh the fragile twins. Getting out her bathroom scales, she gave them a public weigh-in, before the assembled Company. The work having given them a healthy appetite, they had each put on two pounds.

At sixteen, though still around twelve to look at, a private from a nearby army camp stopped the twins on their way to school.
'Haven't you got a pretty sister?' he leered.
There was no doubt that he meant the envied Bonnie. Though the twins were starting at art school in September, adulthood seemed light-years away.

Chapter 5

Behind the bus-stop, facets of light glinted on rain fresh leaves, wind shaken and lit by a flash of sun. On a June day in the nineteen eighties, portfolio in hand, Catherine Robb set off from her home. In a stone faced Edwardian terrace, the steps of its sloping garden seemed steeper these days. Starting to cross the wide road, her hair, bleached corn gold, blew across one eye. For an instant, she saw the rigid steel of the stop sign flow in stem like curves.

Once on the pavement, heart racing, she took stock of the situation. Hand over her right eye, she glanced at the opposite terrace. The whole scene was out of focus, but where her eye settled, hallucinatory curves swayed. Colour at least was normal. Sunlit stone and flower hued gardens had a reality still. Stepping onto a bus, she knew she must see an optician, but which? She recalled a rather too discreet sign she had seen. Nearing the town centre, she turned right. There was the remembered sign, 'A.C. Johnston, Optician'.

Double glass doors topped a flight of stairs. Given the next appointment, she sat down to wait. Glancing around she saw brocaded settees with matching chairs. Their mock mahogany frames had a too dark brilliance. The sight of them stirred a faint memory but it refused to surface...... While waiting, she stared with amusement at a list of opticians. The three A.C. Johnstons had identical initials, presumably passed from father to son. A curious survival, Cath thought, of the old '& Son' tradition. Her father's sign 'H. Hunt & Son' had long since gone.

The receptionist called
'Go through and turn right Mrs Robb – Mr Cliff will see you now.'
Mr Cliff, presumably A.C. Johnson Junior, examined both her eyes. He spoke of a loss of vision in one eye, usually seen in the elderly.
'What have you been doing to get this at your age?' he asked, with a puzzling hint of the suggestive.
Thoughts of sexually transmitted diseases flashed through Cath's mind. As she made no reply, he waved a hand in dismissal, adding

'See your GP about this.'.

Picking up her belongings, Cath made her way to a shop in a small side street. Its sign 'H.G. Kent, Leeds Building Society' would soon be replaced by one of her own. Kent ushered her in.
'Come in come in, beautiful day, isn't it? Have you brought me the work?'
Effusive as always, he hovered over her while she opened her portfolio. Cath was highly conscious of his physical presence. He looked worn and dilapidated, uncared for like his room. She felt that, in spite of his ready tongue, he was essentially an isolate like herself. His appeal was also in certain physical traits. His curly brown hair, his bird like eagerness.

Looking at her work, a sign for the door and several small pieces, he exclaimed
'These are excellent! I must write you a cheque right away.'
Taking a dog eared chequebook from his briefcase, he did so. Though pleased, she saw his enthusiasm as patronising. They weren't so brilliant after all. As he helped her zip up her folder, he promised work for her later. Closing the door, he murmured effervescent good-byes. He seemed drawn to her. Was it, she thought, just part of his sales talk? She fought back images of an open shirt, curling hair spiralling down..... At the thought of her husband Alan's warm beard, a stab of guilt seized her. He had been so distant lately......

Next she boarded a bus to Newcastle, to resume her interrupted day. Though sleepy, she scanned the Tyne valley. Rain and wind gone, the sun poured its gold over the opposite slopes. The shrieking yellow had left the rape fields now, to blend more subtly with surrounding hues. Here and there the sharp geometry of re-afforested pines intruded. Small farm houses appeared with their own tree clusters.

Occasionally, secluded and safe from the trampling feet of incomers like herself, she saw the great home of a landowner. Local contact with such beings was minimal. The only ones she could recall were weddings at Hexham Abbey. She saw glimpses of these weddings, while shopping. Perhaps the grey topper of an elegant youth and his girl, expensively dressed. Their unmistakable tones would fall like an alien rain.

As the bus carried on, the Tyne meandered from view. Cath let sleep take over, as isolated terraces forecast Newcastle. She then made her way to her favourite restaurant. The White Friars was a mediaeval building, now refurbished. Among spotlights and greenery, old machines were part of the decor. From the self-service area, she bought a sandwich and a cup of their excellent coffee. She took a seat at her favourite table – one of two quarry-tiled ones under a window. Settling down, she began planning her afternoon's work at the Hanover Press nearby. She must get on with her prints.

She had recently printed the first edition, in her series titled 'Cloned in the Twenties and Thirties'. These were based on photographs and memories of her twinned childhood. She aimed to evoke the hand coloured photos of the period. The first print featured her father and mother, he in Masonic apron and she in Twenties style beads. Its caption retold a family story, that her teetotal father's celibratory port had later resulted in the birth of the twins.

As she ate in the cafe, Cath mulled over ideas for more prints. Through spicy scent and the clatter of trays, her thoughts ran on. She must do some work on her mother's breakdown. The mental hospital had cast a long shadow. What about her first sight of its grim exterior? Or perhaps the start of the breakdown, her mother's making of a too small pie. The horror of it, infinitely small on the vast white cloth, hungry diners looking on.

Another print she just had to do would feature a Masonic Christmas party. She would base it on a photo with a strange fey quality. Santa Claus on a sledge had sister Bonnie as a fairy and a boy elf carrying a lantern. At either side stood a beefeater, behind were the partying crowd. It had given her the idea for the series. After illustrating poems for a magazine, she had felt an urge for her own theme. It had to be different, unique. Looking through an album, the party scene had jumped from the page. Why not use the family as theme? She decided to make a start on the party and hurried to Hanover Square.

Only two sides were standing of a once elegant square, the others a casualty of war. An area of green with paint peeled railings faced the houses. Pigeons searched its faded shrubs, near a seat spreading curlicued feet. The once bombed area was empty of all but a bulldozer, near a sign for a new building scheme.

At number seven, Cath clambered into a basement, now the Hanover Press printmaking workshop. The whitewashed cellar had a variety of presses, plus acid baths and a hot plate.

'Hi there Cath!' called out Sheena Rama, head of the litho department. Sheena, dressed totally in black as were most, had just returned from a trip to India to study dance styles there. She was at work on four-colour stone litho prints. They subtly blended Hindu temples and their dance forms. Their colour recalled to Cath the Manchester studios she had worked in – turquoise, tyrian, brilliant rose Bengal.

Others there were students feverishly finishing last minute work for college shows. Maturer figures were Roy Clements, an old established member, and Max Vernon, who ran the etching department. Tall introspective, he was continually throwing back his waist long hair, dated now. Eager to get his work into a prestigious London gallery, he had given little attention recently to organising classes. As he collected his prints into his portfolio, Cath thought them brilliant. A composite of photo and litho, they brought out the amateur in other work around. New members soon drifted away from the press, bewildered by technicalities and art jargon. Cath could sympathise with them. Anyone not at art college could be patronised or ignored. When asked, she had mentioned diplomas and design studio work, but the same people still queried

'Are you doing a foundation course?'

Cath unloaded her gear and began work on an enlarged version of the Masonic party photo. At rustling papers heads lifted, including a male one, pink with a satin sheen. Seeing only a middle-aged woman, interest flagged.

'How are you going on then?' Cath asked Roy Clements.

'Great', he said excitedly, 'I've just been given a commission to illustrate a wholefoods cook book.'

'Brilliant! How much work will there be?' asked Cath.
'Work in colour and black and white.' he said. 'Wild herbs in their natural setting., plus a cover.'
Cath was pleased for Roy, though suppressing a pang of envy. Overheard conversations hinted at his working all hours to meet deadlines. She had first met him a year ago, as a member of his wood engraving course at the press.

Cath added new figures to the left on the Masonic party plate, to centre the sledge with its flanking beef eaters. The prints in the series had a drawn frame around, with details straying over the edge. On this plate she floated a Spanish shawl over the frame. Her concentration relaxing, she heard voices talking about the meeting at six. She had arranged with Alan to stay late.

People were starting to pack up. She looked at her watch, five thirty-five. She got out her folder and cleared up her things, quickly putting on lipstick. Somebody got out a bottle of plonk and she accepted a glass. As she drank, the ruby red of her mouth left its double, imprinted on the rim.
'Straight out of 'Casablanca'' whispered a clean faced young woman.
In eighty two, lipstick was out. Feeling apart from the young crowd, Cath thought
'Well at least I'm a paid up member, which is more than some of them are.'

The meeting began with Sheena Rama as Chair, Max Vernon, normally the Chair, having quietly disappeared.
'The purpose of this meeting' began Sheena, 'is to discuss the objectionable behaviour of a certain staff member.'
She raised her voice as a murmur began.
'Namely Max Vernon, who was asked to be here but refused. The complaint is that a member in another room heard Max showing only his own work to a gallery rep. Coming specially from London, the rep went back without seeing any other members' work.'
'His teaching's not what it should be,' piped someone 'He does all your work instead of showing you how!'
'That's right!' said another. 'He cares about nobody's work but his

own.'

After more comment, nothing being concluded, some members began drifting away.

It was the first Cath had heard of the problem, but she wasn't surprised. Max had charged her twenty pounds for tuition. Later she found it hadn't gone to the press. Also he had done all the processes himself, not giving her time to practice. No-one came to Max's defence. All agreed he should resign. As the meeting broke up, groups drifted to a pub and Cath walked on alone.

Out in the square, a faint scent spread from the little park. Shadowed trees darkened the few parked cars. Making her way over the building site, Cath sought the White Friars restaurant again. As she pushed open its new pine doors, a spicy aroma mingled with dampness from the ageing stones. She couldn't afford a hot meal, just biscuits with cheese and a coffee.

As she ate, she tried to push away images of vision loss. Closing her right eye, she saw again the strange world. High arched windows swayed in plantlike curves. Hoping the other eye wouldn't be affected, she tried to regain hope. Hadn't she read that few of the blind had full vision loss? Leaving her food, she exited into the cool fresh air.

Street lamps glowed as Cath looked towards Hanover Square. The tea-rose sky faded into green, then deepening blue at its farther end. A doorway lit up, as elderly men walked in beneath a sign, 'F.E.P.O.W. Club', ex-prisoners of war, she assumed. Cath wondered why they chose this area for their meetings. With its many Chinese restaurants, banks, a supermarket, it was the centre of the Chinese community. Surely this would be a reminder to the old men of their Japanese captors, so alike in appearance.

Cath felt the Chinese gave a cosmopolitan air to the place. Hearing a commotion outside a restaurant, she looked through an archway and saw a crowd. Over their heads, a swirling dragon fixed her with the hallucinatory glare of its ball eyes.

PART 2

Chapter 6

Two heads just surfaced above the enormous desk on its raised platform. The twins weighed up Miss Owen their Art teacher, as she opened a large expensive book. She wore her dark hair in a low bun. Unfashionably bra-less, with floating scarves in purples and greens, to them she seemed a model of the spinster school mistress. They saw her life as much more a 'fate worse than death' than those of the fallen women in grandma's old novels. Glancing at each other, they suppressed giggles. They had noted a lump of face cream not quite rubbed in, on her Grecian but rosy nose. This effort at make-up was because she was taking them to Huddersfield School of Art.

Realising the twins' ignorance of the arts in general, Veronica Owen had advised their parents to let them stay for a year in the sixth. Harold and Edna had agreed but had given way under Cath's protests. She was desperate to get away from the restrictive girls' school, too much like home. Cora had a stronger bond with their parents, though of an over dependent kind.

The large book on Veronica's desk was Arthur Rackham's 'Book of Fairies' She let the twins leaf through its illustrations for some time. The delicately winged creatures floating through melancholy twilight trees were evocative of their childhood dream world, but beautiful though it was, they wished to move on. Veronica had worked in stage design at a London theatre. An Associate of Royal College, she could have drawn them out of their naive world.

On the bus journey to Art School, the twins felt embarrassed as locals stared at Miss Owen. Looking as if transplanted from Bloomsbury, she was a novelty in the hidebound little town. As, following in her wake, the twins entered the art school, fear of the new slowed them to a crawl. Hearing their tread diminishing, Veronica turned to see her charges trailing behind.

'Come along now girls!' she called in annoyance, as they hurried to her side.

However, the interview with the headmaster was not the ordeal they had imagined. Mildly amused, his smile put them at their ease and as he showed them round the various departments, their interest grew. There was the painting room with its heavy smell of turps. Next door, rich fabrics in mainly reds and browns hung on a rail near jars and pans of dye.

On reaching home, for once they made news with an account of their day. The Bohemian Miss Owen's over hasty make-up had Bonnie hysterical, but their father commented

'If you'd any sense, you'd have had a year in the Sixth with that woman.'

Still, since laying down the law to Bonnie, with results little short of disastrous, he had decided that the twins could work things out for themselves.

After tea, on the large settee with their homework, the twins whispered to each other

'All dressed up to go dreaming....'

They eyed Bonnie's fair hair, piled high in front with shoulder length curls. She wore a black hat with her 'little black dress', plus the inevitable seamed stockings and high heels.

'Has he owt?' Harold had asked, having met new boy friend Fred for the first time. It seemed he was no better off financially than her other amours, though he was generous. The twins at least thought so, as he spent his sweet ration buying them boxes of chocolates. They gladly accepted the sweets, though they knew it was only to get well in with Bonnie. As she and Fred left for a night on the town, each twin sat munching a Fry's chocolate cream and wondering if the day would ever come, when they would set off, in high heels and make-up, each draped over the arm of some marvellous man.......

At three o'clock the next morning, Cath awoke to find Bonnie undressing and crying, quietly so as not to disturb her sisters. Cath pretended sleep, but next minute the door burst open and their father rushed in armed with a coat hanger.

'What time d' you call this?' he bawled.

Clutching the opening of his striped pyjamas in one hand, with the other he rained down blows on Bonnie, until she snatched it from him. Throughout the scene, he never let go of the clutched pyjamas.

'If you'd like to know' sobbed Bonnie, 'I had a late night because I'll be leaving on Friday. I've joined the Wrens and I won't be back!'

'I'm so sorry Love......' was all Harold could say, as he crept out exhausted.

Yellow cheeks hanging like a bloodhound's, emotions swamped him. Guilt at his outburst vied with a new pride in Bonnie. She had always been the only one to stand up to him.

Harold had never felt close to his son, but since he had begun lead burning, they seemed even further apart. Osbert would come home in his overalls, then get dressed up and slink out, God knew where. Harold felt dubious about his son's re-opening the business post war, but he hoped the good will would enable him to carry on. To further provide for him, he made a will, leaving three sevenths of his property to Osbert and one seventh to each of the girls.

He had earlier hoped that Osbert would become a Freemason. Now, aware of his son's amused contempt for the Brotherhood, he had instead asked his son-in-law to apply for membership. Harold often played chess with his son-in-law. With Larry's record as a local cricketer and golfer, Harold felt he would take the matter seriously. Larry felt pleased and flattered. Always more at home with his own sex than with women, he looked forward with relish to joining. Especially to the occasions it would provide for the exercise of his wit and charm in an atmosphere not unlike his cricket club. Though he didn't admit this to himself, the wearing of the apron and the dazzling decorations appealed to certain homosexual leanings. He had always had some close friend who, like himself, never admitted to such feelings.

During the holidays, the twins spent a day in the mill haunted countryside with friends. Friends of Cora's that is, as Cath's greater introspection was attractive to few. The four of them set off early from Huddersfield, seated in front on the top deck of a double-decker bus. The talk centred on their approaching new lives as students; the twins at art school and their friends as nurses at the Royal Infirmary.

As the bus pulled up, a girl got out of an opposite seat. As she clattered down metal capped stairs, they noticed her face, flattened, with a hollowed out bridge to the nose.

'She's just like Bonnie's friend Shirley!' said Cora.

'The image.' agreed Cath.

'You know what's the cause of that, don't you?' remarked Iris.

'No, What on earth do you mean?' asked Cora.

'It's caused by a venereal disease, syphilis.', went on Iris.

'You can't get to look like that just through going with a lad!' giggled Brenda, but Cora was horrified.

'I don't see anything to laugh at!' she exclaimed, 'I'd hate any of my kids to get it.'

She was thinking of Shirley and the comments people made. The twins had heard too many remarks about their asthma, not to sympathise.

'I'm sorry,' said Brenda, anxious to conciliate, 'Some cases are actually quite pretty.'

They passed on to less controversial topics, gazing out of the window at tall weavers cottages rising in layers on the hillside. These were characteristic of Hebden Bridge, where they were to spend their day. Stepping awkwardly from the bus, the twins were surprised to be breathing normally, the pollen count must be low. The sun shone over a fleece of cloud, as the group meandered through a glacial valley. Stepping stones crossed the broadening stream. They paddled out to larger stones and taking sandwiches from carefully hoarded paper bags, they enjoyed food as seldom before.

'Pork Pies with green fat on.' laughed Brenda, but she couldn't put the others off their food or the bottled drinks. From these bottles the discarded straws now formed into boats, sailed on or were trapped in whirlpools, their mossy depths dark with the green of weed. In the shallows a broken sun glinted on hurrying waves. Lying on the bank, the girls gathered small life in jars or rapidly fragmenting bags, mayfly larvae in stony cases, spiders and beetles of the water variety. Low hills shadowed the stream, when they wandered back to the village. The many storied weavers cottages, their windows built to catch most light, flashed faceted rose, as they approached the bus stop. Catching sight of a 'Ladies' sign, they hurried down steps to a reeking interior, where a V.D. poster leapt at them from the walls.

Cora and Cath began their student lives with the rest of the new intake. Their first session, sketching ancient Egyptian borders from copies of a huge tome known as Owen Jones, was voted easy if uninspiring. At break time the class hung about in a corridor in small groups around the radiators. Here they were joined by architectural students, all male except one. Cath thought she recognised a blond boy fleetingly, but couldn't recall from where.

Next came the life class, where a new boy Jim, coloured to his dark fringe at his first sight of a feminine nude.
'These are an unpromising lot.' mused Eric Crowther, lecturer in painting. He strode around, looking at their first feeble efforts at life drawing. The model, fortyish, called by Eric 'the brassy one', was scarcely likely to enthuse. From peroxide waves to vermilion toenails she was covered in sun tan make-up. As she settled into her pose, her drooping breasts swayed unappetisingly. An enormous sticking plaster covered her 'mound of Venus', presumably to save on peroxide.
'Why couldn't they have some fresh young girl, instead of this old bag,' thought Jim, as he struggled to concentrate, his blushes subsiding.

Lunch time arriving, the first years made their way to the canteen. Here they joined a queue. Before a vast assemblage of cups on a white cloth, a tiny woman walked back and forth, tipping a huge teapot between cups. Miraculously not a drop was spilt. As the twins chattered together, trailing behind the others, she snapped
'You need a bomb behind you!' Too shy to join in the general

conversation, Cath got out a book and as she ate, became lost in its world. Cora though shy too made an effort and listened to views on the day so far.

'All those architects, I didn't realise they'd be there!' exclaimed one of the girls Joy, eyes alight. She smoothed down her skirt as if to minimise the generous proportions of hip and thigh.

'You're so right', said another student, Angela, 'It's going to be better than I thought here.' A lovely looking girl, she was part Norwegian.

'Well I came here to work.' another girl, Dot, cut in. With a slight limp, her family had sent her to college instead of the mill. To justify the expense, she knew she had to do well.

The afternoon's fare was more from the great tome Owen Jones. Its pages bulged with the arts of the ancients, Greek, Egyptian and Persian. To the group, the examples were redolent of the museum. They wanted the exciting and new. On the lecturer Clare Booth, Cath commented

'She's a bit of a museum piece herself, like Miss Owen.'

Entering their home that evening, the warmth from Harold's leaky central heating reminded the twins of the break time gatherings around the college radiators. They felt a sense of shame at the way they'd hung back, unable to take part in the talk. As they walked into the front room, their two-year old niece ran up, calling

'Cath-Cora, Cath-Cora' She pulled at their skirts, as they settled on the settee. Her visiting mother Lulu paid the twins no compliments.

'Bony knees and bitten nails!' she carped, 'You'll never get a nice young man!'

'Well Girls, how's your first day?' asked their father, rising from his chair by the fire.

'I've got something for you.' he added. He produced two new drawing boards to replace the old ones they had borrowed from Osbert. The girls faces lit up and then fell. They saw that each board bore the imprint of a rubber stamp, 'H. Hunt & Son Ltd., Plumber and Electrician, 12, Highgate, Huddersfield'. They thanked Harold in subdued tones, but the emotional confusion the gift stirred up was too much for Cath. She ran up to her bedroom, wiping away tears with the back of her hand. As Cora followed, Harold muttered to Edna, setting the table,

'What's wrong with the little buggers now? When have they ever shown any gratitude!' Edna put up a restraining hand, seeing the anger darken his face. Relegating her task to Lulu, she followed the twins to their room.

'Why can't you be thankful when you're given something?' she exploded.

'You must realise by now that your father's very ill and hasn't to be excited.' Sorrow and guilt fought with rage at the rubber stamped logos, as Cath struggled to push back the tears.

'I just wanted a plain board like everyone else.' she wept. 'Anyway, now everyone will know that Dad's a plumber and we'll get laughed at again!' Her anger cooling, Edna began to sympathise with the twins, putting her arms around them. They shrank from the close contact, following her down the stairs.

'Plumbing is nothing to be ashamed of. None of those students are out of the top drawer.' Edna continued. She was anxious to pacify them before facing Harold. She was relieved to see that he was smiling as he talked to his grandson, just in from school. Bonnie and Osbert began to argue,

'I'm first in the bathroom, I'm meeting a smashing new guy!'

'It's my turn for a bath, I'm seeing Betty.'

'Not before time. She's been phoning for weeks.'

During the next months at college, the break time chat around the radiators continued. Sometimes a large crowd of architects would collect, at other times just a few. As the group broke up one morning, a grinning student gave Joy a package. Opening it, in the secrecy of the 'Ladies', Joy blushed furiously, at what she saw. Two joined pans from a toy scale had ribbons attached at the sides. The meaning eluded the twins until the next day, when Joy and Angela each appeared, wearing pointed bra's. After this all the girls took to wearing them, but Cora and Cath, unable to buy a small enough size, made their own out of ribbon and handkerchiefs.

Joy as 'sweater girl' must have pleased her tormentor. For a month, the two were inseparable, then the boy drifted away. For several days, Joy's features registered grief. Clare Booth remarked 'That girl has wider mood swings than any I've come across. Within a week, Joy was all smiles and excitement again, with several boys pressing for dates. Angela too was in great demand from boys both in and out of the college. Dot often worked through her break times. She didn't agree with

'all this kissing, passing germs on!' Sniggers of Hop Along Cassidy followed her dragging foot, but she slammed back

'It's a pity some folks don't get on with their work! Some of us 'll have to earn our keep.'

Cath and Cora continued to hang on to the fringe of the crowd around their radiator. To the amusement of their parents, Cath developed a contralto voice, which no one knew she possessed. Her deep throated versions of current hits, such as

'Thrills run up and down my spine, Aladdin's lamp is mine....', would float from the upper regions of the house. Cora, hearing the mocking laughter, carried on singing school choir songs, in her sweet soprano voice.

The twins took to frequenting cinemas on Saturday nights. Their favourite fare being the concoctions churned out by J. Arthur Rank, particularly those featuring Stewart Granger, in his darkly romantic period. Also among their favourites were nostalgic American productions such as 'Now Voyager' starring Bette Davis. Her transformation from ugly duckling to swan particularly appealed to them. Sitting, enclosed by the darkness, each secretly felt that all that was missing was a boyfriend beside her, instead of the ever-present clone.

Failing this, Cora decided that an unreturned love was better than none and developed a crush on their fresh faced classmate Jim. Not to be outdone, Cath kept an eye open for someone to fall for. As it happened, she made a less suitable choice. She picked on tall sleek Don Blair. His amused attitude towards her, only strengthened her attachment. One break, beside the radiator, when the theme was religious films, Cath boobed.

'My favourite was Bing Crosby as a priest in that musical,' Laughter interrupted her, especially from her idol.

'Not a religious film.' he grinned, sophistication itself. Aware of her feelings, he would sometimes suggest to the other architects

'Shall I take her up into sketch club?', (The attic room, used by couples for generations.) Cath put the answered 'No's' down to her hated naivete.

One night months later, she waited for Cora at the college entrance. A heavy man got out of a car, wide brimmed hat pulled over one eye. From the darkness Don Blair ran into his arms. As the man looked up, Cath saw his face, lipsticked, powdered and rouged. Then blackness as the door closed. She realised that everyone knew! Hints such as

'You want to forget about him, he won't take you to the pictures.' assumed a new meaning now.

Disappointment took a grip on Cath. Her pace slowed down, especially in the life class. She'd sit staring at the model, afraid to put down a stroke.

'Just get something down on the paper' Eric Crowther counselled, 'You'll learn by your mistakes.' Cath found this hard to follow. The others all seemed to be racing ahead. She felt left behind, defeated. Cora's passion for Jim settled into a friendship. At lunch breaks they talked about books, especially Mervin Peak's, which they eagerly swapped. Hints of Peak's illustrations crept into Jim's work.

After the Christmas break, a new face turned up at the Art School. Invalided from the forces, he was recovering from war traumas. Called Ted Marshall, he was the new lecturer in illustration and textiles. He suggested that Jim should take illustration, while the girls should do screen printed textiles. Cath had wanted to paint with Eric Crowther. She kept this quiet as she saw her work lapse. Though there were rumours that Ted had had some kind of breakdown, it was far from obvious. In fact, his enthusiasm brought new hope to the students. They discarded the old block prints, when he brought in the new silk screens. Their colour sense and drawing blossomed, as he led them towards a floral based style.

'These'll make great Dirndle skirts!' enthused Joy.

'No coupons either!' added Angela.

Cath tried to feel more upbeat, watching escapist movies in 'Glorious Technicolor' Cora preferred to stay home and read. Tonight's film featured the song 'Nothing but Blue Skies do I see' Sentimentalised, it totally lost the subtlety of the earlier black and white version she had seen, featuring Alice Faye. Leaving the Ritz, images of blond curls and parted red lips against skies of boring blue vanished with hardly a trace. Back at home, a long groan drifted from her father's room.

Some weeks later, Edna, struggling up stairs with her mother-in-law's tray, sensed an unusual silence. Entering the bedroom, she found the old lady dead. The family showed little reaction, as Grandma had been bed-ridden for some time. Cora shed a few tears, but Cath felt little. A memory surfaced, of scrambling down from her grandmother's knee, refusing the closeness. The coffin lay in the cold drawing room for days. The wrinkled drawn back skin suggested the skeleton beneath. Harold felt it wouldn't be too long before he joined his mother, as they buried her in the large family grave.

Depressed on the morning bus, Cath wondered why a young girl, enormously fat, her leg in a calliper, was beaming with apparent joy. As the twins wheezed their way up the college stairs, late for their class, life drawing had already begun. They entered to find they were under discussion.

'Those twins aren't a bit alike, one's sweet and fresh and the other's hard and worn.' said the model. No prizes for guessing which twin's which.' Cath thought, as they disrupted the class with the scraping of easels.

As break time, Angela announced in the 'Ladies' that she was meeting a boy that night.

'Don't mention it to the architects', she cautioned. There were still one or two good-lookers among them that she hadn't sampled yet. The date lined up for that night was due back at his army unit at three a.m.

'He's really something!', she told the girls. Flicking back her near blond hair, she speedily crushed on her lipstick. Bare brown legs above high heels, she set off down a flight of stairs. Slipping on the well-worn steps, she twisted her ankle. Scorning a taxi home, she sat all afternoon in pain, determined to get to her date. Cath who had planned a lone cinema visit, offered to share a taxi.

While waiting, Cath ventured

'I envy you Angela, couldn't you teach me some tricks about boys.....?'

'You know Cath you're attractive, you look like Barbara Stanwick,' Angela surprisingly answered, 'It's just that you're far too serious.' Flattered to be compared to a star, Cath's reactions were mixed, when she thought of Miss Stanwivk's roles.

'Boys like a girl to be fun.' went on Angela, but Cath longed for more than laughter – an intense relationship, like she had known with Cora in childhood.....

Tooting its horn, the taxi arrived. As they drew up at the meeting place, a fresh faced youth emerged from a portico's shade. He sleeked back a forelock of delicate gold, its colour intensified by his corporal's khaki. Her foot now swollen hugely, Angela staggered to the base of a pillar and seating herself there, smiled and chattered to the soldier.

'Let's get you to the hospital.' he said protectively. Stifling an envious pang, Cath decided the paragon was worth the suffering, as she made her lone way to the Lyceum Cinema.

Chapter 7

'There'll be blue birds over the white cliffs of Dover.....' The too familiar voice of Vera Lynn belted out the schmaltzy lyric. Mocked as it often was, today cynicism was out. It was V.E. Day. The 'Day to Remember' had begun with the sun breaking through a rosy mist. Around ten, with money for drinks, and plenty of sandwiches, the twins set out for the celebrations in Thorndale Park. They felt at their best in pale pink linen bordered with navy, sewn by themselves with rationed material. First they made for the 'Holidays at Home' show, in the makeshift theatre. Eyes wide, they watched the children on stage. A small girl and two small boys were the first. In brilliant green, twirling a feather duster, the vivacious child led her followers. Their rendition of

'The waiter and the porter and the upstairs maid.' filled the park. A series of wartime hits were followed by several Carmen Mirandas and a top hatted chorus line. Then the twins drifted away from the crowd, in search of their childhood haunts.

They found the old conservatory, in its enclosure of flowering shrubs, now deserted and forlorn, its windows broken.

'I wonder if they'll repair it now the war's over.' mused Cora.

They remembered the richness of forms brilliant among glossy leaves, hinting at bliss half recalled...... A massing of tropical blooms, lilies orchids, vibrant or starkly white, was imaged by each of the girls.

'Remember the jam tart flowers?' they simultaneously asked, as they wandered off along paths bordered by flowering trees.

Near the bandstand, denuded still of flashy uniforms and blaring brass, was an ice-cream cart, dragged from obscurity for the festive day. Joining the queue, the twins stared at the bright faced girl, dressed in red white and blue. She moved with a natural ease and rhythm. As she smiled and filled cones, her ease was foreign to the cloned pair, but greatly longed for.

There was great excitement later, as the lights were turned on all over the town. They almost outshone the sun, as it lowered in a clear pale sky. As the crowds grew thicker, the twins continued to wander, hoping faintly for a hint of romance. The nearest they got to it were shouts from a couple of not so young foreign soldiers on a seat.

'Ze little twins. Come 'ere, Come 'ere!' 'We give you good time!'

One smiled, showing broken teeth, while the other winked suggestively. Empty bottles clinked at their feet. Shrugging at the twins' lack of response, they lit up and opened yet more beers. As Cathy and Cora hurried away, the ice-cream girl appeared again, linking arms with a troop of friends, their eyes bright as the lamp lit scene. They loudly chorused

'Roll me over, in the clover, roll me over, lay me down and do it again!', drowning out the lingering bars of

'I'm gonna get lit up when the lights go on in London!'

Wishing they could join some part of the festive crowd but not knowing how, the twins made their way through the flag festooned streets to their home.

Cath had taken to 'Modern' art. and had picked up a copy of Clive Bell's 'Significant Form'. Its reduction of everything in painting to pure form chimed in with the bleakness of her present outlook. She bought or borrowed the small number of books available on the subject, all on abysmal paper. She still had a sneaking preference for the block prints she had done the previous term before the new lecturer's arrival. Now the blocks were gathering dust on a corner of a shelf, as screen printing was in vogue. Her design, consisting of circles and sweeping curves, seemed to her more in line with the modernists than the delicate floral borders they were working on with Ted. Cath's line drawing and figure composition gradually improved, though Cora's were still in advance. Eric Crowther's outburst at the beginning of term had spurred them into an all-out effort.

'You've no taste, no imagination and you can't draw!' he had remarked, as they suspected he did every year.

Much too soon, the students were in the midst of the intermediate exam. In the architectural section, the invigilator tactfully went out, as they stared at each other in panic, faced with the problem of drawing their own college.

'We'll never draw that gothic monstrosity!' whispered Joy.

'Think of all the pinnacles and fancy bits. It'll take hours.' said Cora.

'I've an idea.....' Jim suggested, 'Why don't we draw the new library?'

'Brilliant! Nothing to it but that Epstein type sculpture.' gasped Joy. All agreed until Dot broke in

'I've practised the front of this college for hours and I'm going to draw it. You do what you like.'

As there was no changing her mind, she drew her version and they drew theirs, though worried that the differences may be a problem.

'We needn't worry about that,' said Cath, 'Huddersfield isn't on the map!'

When it came to drawing and painting the design that they would later print on actual fabric, Cath had what seemed to the staff a mental aberration. She used the design from her old block print instead of the new floral styles. Ted was livid as Cath would have to use her old block and different dyes, though she saw a twinkle in Clare Booth's eye.

When the morning for printing arrived, Cath's mind seemed totally empty. She started one manoeuvre then another, got dye all over her pan handles and generally behaved like one of Skinners most neurotic rats.

'You know Cath, I sometimes think you're a bit simple!' exclaimed Joy, sharing a bench with Cath. When Cath had printed the background, instead of the intended rich Indian red, it gradually dried into the depressing brown of a school room desk. The exam results showed that Cath and Joy had failed, while everyone else had passed. Though Cath tried hard to take Eric Crowther's advice and 'take it in her stride', she felt crushed by the blow. She suspected that partnering her had influence Joy's failure too. Cora tried to comfort, but the sweetness of her smile was cloying in the extreme.

Cath's cinema visits tailed off, third programme listening taking their place. Mozart and Haydn appealed to her mainly, the romantics being too full of the sentiment she now avoided. She tried to feel the aesthetic emotion vaunted by Clive Bell in his 'Significant Form' as she leafed through paperbacks on Henry Moore et al. Peering at Old Master reproductions, she would try to reduce them also to the confines of Bell's purist theories. Cath genuinely liked the work of Stanley Spencer, also loved by Eric Crowther. Strongly influenced by Spencer was a series of murals by Crowther in the local library, on early industrial crises.

Cora was mad about a recent book, 'The Pre-Raphaelite tragedy' Though the book aroused Cath's interest, she resolutely crushed these sympathies, feeling that Bell would not approve. The college saw Art Nouveau and Victoriana as the essence of bad taste. When staff showed a piece of Art Nouveau, a book jacket or music cover, as an example of decadence, Cath would have to try hard to deny the curious attraction it had for her. Cora just liked what appealed to her and made no attempt to intellectualise about it. Though Jim Walton never became emotionally involved with her, they would have long friendly discussions on painting and current illustration. During these he would throw out hints about Cath's intellectual snobbery.

Cath continued her reading, it seemed easier than personal contact. Having no love affairs to reveal she felt she was prying when the others revealed theirs, such as Joy's confessions to her priest on 'sins of touch' That seemed to be as far as Joy had progressed, though Angela, Cath gathered, was much more experienced.

On some days, Cath had stayed reading at lunch time. The architects would drift in and talk about the absent girls, ignoring Cath's presence as totally as if she weren't there.
'She's common' was their reference to Angela's free and easy style, especially from those who had taken advantage. For some time Joy had dated Ellis an architect, a public school boy. Already plump and prosperous looking, a place was waiting at his father's firm. In buoyant mood, Joy flew in Ellis's sports car from one excitement to another. In depression she recalled stronger feelings for other men. As she strolled by on one of her highs, an architect muttered
'Can't stand that woman – the way she looks hungry for men....'

The next year's new intake at the art school included Cath and Joy, as they were to repeat the intermediate year. Cora and the other successes would take their finals in three year's time. It seemed strange to the twins not to be together in class, but it allowed them to develop as individuals. They still continued to meet at the radiators between classes. One break-time, Don Blair excitedly told the crowd of a new musical film he'd just seen, 'Up in Arms'.

'There's a bloke in it – Danny Kaye, you must see him!' he enthused. Before long, Kaye had become a craze, Joy doing brilliant impressions.

As they hung about at the edge of their group, the twins were excruciatingly aware of every quirk of each other's behaviour, as if in some cruel mirror. Edna, trying to 'make do and mend' had made each twin a pair of the new slacks. She made the two pairs from one pair of Harold's enormous trousers. Unfortunately the garments had turned out too tight, revealing to each clone her emaciated self. While wearing them a shock awaited the pair as, going downstairs, an architect called out

'Have a look twins! There's your portrait at the bottom of the stairs!' Trying to look nonchalant, they were unprepared for their first sight of the inmates of Belsen!

It wasn't long before Angela cast her eye on a swarthy looking architect, who she fancied as a permanent acquisition. He was soon unable to give her up in spite of, or because of, her known propensities. She acquired a girlfriend from another department. Ordinary at first glance, she had a brooding sensuality around lips and eyes. Avoiding her old friend Joy, at lunch breaks the two would make for an empty table. From here they would weigh up the males in the queue, giving the eye to any that appealed.

On one break, Cath was as usual engrossed in a book, a reductionist work by Roger Fry. She looked up as a shadow hovered over the page. A smiling Angela asked

'Cath could I borrow your book for a sec?' Cath felt the group around her bristle, but secretly she longed to extract, in exchange for the book, an entry to Angela's luxurious world. She handed over the book saying

nothing. As Angela moved off to her pretence of reading, Joy exploded.
'Why did you give it to her? She's just taking advantage!'
'She's making a fool of you!' hissed Dot. Cath could think of no answer, as men hovered like bees around Angela.

Jim too had developed a passion for her. Her hair, carelessly tossing, haunted his work. Venturing to ask for a date, he got a laughing refusal. In the confines of the Gents he questioned an architect, Brian.
'She's the tart of the town man! You want to have nothing to do with her.' he was advised.
'If it's experience you want Kid, she's your answer I should think. I know nothing about women myself.' added Don. Brian turned on him,
'Don't tempt the kid, you don't know what Angela's got! She's been with everything trousered!'
'Including you?' smiled Don.
'Not a chance!' returned Brian. Jim slunk back to his class, cheeks burning.

In moments of gloom Cath often recalled what had suddenly appeared on a country drive with her parents. Rounding a corner, there had flashed into view the immense frontage of Thorpe Lees Hall, the local mental institution.
'Do we have to go past this place Harold?' Edna had asked,
'It brings back all I want to forget'
'You've never been in there.' snapped Harold.
'No, but they all look the same.' Edna faltered. Such clues added to Cath's suspicions, fuelled by her father's repeated
'Cath's too much like her mother......' Topping the hospital's blackened facade were hideous cupolas around a central clock tower. Stark against menacing cloud, the image continually haunted Cath, try as she might to forget it. Often tears brimmed, but she forced them back. To her, that was for cowards.

Sickened with the sentimental in films, she now hoped comedy would banish her blues. Cora didn't care for films, so Cath went alone to see 'Walter Mitty'. She had been right. Kaye's non stop antics and colourful costumes cleared her mind. Still early in the evening, in heightened mood she turned along New South Road. Tall lamps lit tree shaded gothic facades, or the sturdy columns of neo-classic. To her surprise she and Cora now had entry to what in their childhood had seemed the 'palaces of dream'.

Lulu and Larry had recently rented a flat in one of these dream homes. Cath was on her way to join Cora there. Breathless after the walk, she saw the name 'Ellersly' carved on a nearing gatepost. Through sparse leafed trees a turreted window glowed. Mounting the steps and ringing the neatly labelled bell, her heart raced as the great door opened and Cora ushered her in. Shoes echoing on mosaic tiles, they entered a long rectangular room. A huge stone fireplace threw out a pleasant warmth. Spanned by a gothic arch, a few brass ornaments looked lost on its heavy mantle. At each side of a many arched window hung curtains of Indian red, brought in from the tenants previous home. A thirties leaf design, they looked at odds with the enormous room. A few rugs and a small carpet left bare most of the stone flagged floor. Lulu had plans for refurbishing the place in sumptuous style, but doubted if Larry would part with the money. She had none of her own, having been politely forced out of her wartime job in a typing pool.

'Cath have a look at this!' Cora said, unfolding a copy of the local paper, as they flopped down among cushions on the leather settee. Cath looked in amazement at Cora's design. Here in black and white, she recalled its lemon and lime spirals on a cream linen ground. The V&A were to exhibit it as an example of contemporary design.

'How fantastic!' she enthused, trying not to think of her work at that time, the hideous thing that had failed her. She must get herself together she thought, though she felt she was catching up now.

'Well I'm pleased one of us is getting somewhere at least,' she said. She studied the rest of the paper, while Cora read 'Brave New World', passed on to her by Cath.

'What do you think of these clones?' Cora asked. It was the first time they had heard the word. Laughing, they visualised a great horde of Coras and Caths rushing through factory gates to meet a corresponding tribe of handsome identical males.

'What's that Miss Carter, a background of vomit?' asked Eric Crowther, glancing over Dot's latest production. The class trooped out and after gossiping at the radiators, piled back into the classroom for life study. The new model from Central Europe was already in his pose as they dawdled in, to a scraping of chairs. The lecturer being late, they all sat chatting until the model made them sit up with a start. Leaping from his seat he suddenly yelled

'I've sat before Europe's finest artists and I'm not sitting here for bloody Yorkshire tykes!' He dressed and was gone before anyone could think of an answer.

Cath came out early, missing it all, as she was due at the local Infirmary. In spite of his illness, Harold had watched her staring into space.

'That one's too much like her mother.' he told Lulu. He had set up an appointment, though Edna had hoped things would cure themselves. As usual she was overruled. Entering the hospital, Cath passed along seemingly endless corridors, clinical smells combining with worse. She found herself in a room where a white-coated male smiled patronisingly down. No couch was visible as she had previously supposed. Seating himself, the doctor began

'So you've been feeling down in the dumps,' in a tone more suited to a child.

'How about boy friends, are they a problem?' he asked.

'More the lack of them.' Cath thought, making no answer.

'Off you go now!' he ended later, 'We'll send you another appointment.'

Chapter 8

Silencing the alarm, wearily Edna gave the twins their first call. It usually took three before they were up. She'd had to put up with sex from Harold the night before. It was far from enjoyable these days. She couldn't bring herself to refuse him sex, his only pleasure now, living as he did on boiled rice and hardly leaving the house. She had experienced nothing but basic intercourse. When she had timidly suggested variety, Harold had sneered
'That's for perverts and pansies!'

With increasing pain, Harold found himself letting out groans that they heard downstairs. For weeks he had brooded over a way of quitting life naturally. Now he had the answer.
'I feel a bit better today Love,' he smiled, with an assumed breeziness, 'I think I'll go down to the golf club and watch them play. I'll be back at lunch-time.' Edna was astonished.
'But you haven't driven the car for weeks Harold. You won't play will you? It could kill you!'
'I'll do what I like.' he said, tight lipped. Dragging himself up on now spindly legs, the loose flesh of his face swung, as he crossed the back garden to his garage. There the unused shelter seemed to mock him with its uselessness. Photographed in front of it, and no air raids! There might be another photo of him in the paper soon.......

At the golf club it was a marvellous day for March. There was no one he knew there, since he hadn't played golf for some months. Reluctantly, a stranger at the bar agreed to play eighteen holes with him. Hole after hole Harold drove himself on, shaking and sweating, in the grip of his pain. It must have been at about the eleventh hole, that the club flew out of his hands. Eyes staring as the sun described a great arc, he slumped at the edge of a bunker. He was dead on arrival at the infirmary.

The funeral arrived, with its trail of hardly known relatives. Edna wore her shabby black dress, the twins new black coats.

'At last I'll get a new outfit.' thought Lulu guiltily, sick of coupons and doing without. Bonnie looked smart in her Wren's uniform. Trinity Church on New South Road was large, but not large enough for the family, as they elbowed their way through crowds of Freemasons. When Edna reached the front, the great stained window swam through her tears. The service ended with a speech from no less a person than the Masonic Lodge's Worshipful Master.

'Our brother was known for his work in the community.' he went on.

'On the Public Assistance and Watch Committees (sniggers) he served the town well.....'

After a cold collation at the Spotted Cow, drink flowed, though not for the twins.

'Poor old Dad,' Bonnie commented from behind her gin and lime, 'it was some oration. Pity he didn't scatter more largesse at home.' Cath piped

'I'll never forget the fever hospital. All the kids but me had their own bags of oranges. I got just one from a sack that he generously supplied for all!' Bonnie carried on

"'Boots for the Bairns', but if we wanted something the answer was 'No!'" Lulu joined in

'Those Masons should see how he hit us! I was black and blue after Holmfirth Sing!'

'Just before I joined up,' Bonnie added, 'he hit me with a coat hanger for coming home late.'

'Poor Dad,' put in Cora 'he was so weak you snatched the hanger away from him....' She began to cry as, shamefaced, they ordered more drinks.

Harold's will left the house and a small income to Edna. He had divided the rest of his estate into sevenths, one each for the girls and three for his son. Osbert also inherited what was left of the business, lying fallow for post war regrowth. His confidence, continually undermined by his father, seemed hardly up to rebuilding the firm. Since his war work ended, he had run a simple man and boy operation from the shop.

Edna carried on as usual it seemed to the twins. Though without extra help now, the house looked untidy and dust gathered. It never occurred to them to do any housework When opening a drawer, Cath saw a strange insect crawling along the sheets. She blew up.

'What on earth's that Mum? This place is getting to be the pits!' she shouted.

'I'm sorry Love.' Edna muttered, turning away, but not before Cath had seen tears.

Their fellow students had read Harold's obituary.

'What will you do now?' and 'What sort of job will you look for?' they asked. Taking all for granted, the spoiled pair assumed they would carry on with their course. After a conference, the family found funds for them to do so.

Cora had begun to notice that all was not well with their mother. Edna would lethargically prepare the evening meal and place it on the table. Leaving her food, she would sit staring into space, eyelids drooping and studded with tears. Osbert was out most nights and said little. Sometimes the twins would go with Edna to lunch or to a theatre, but she didn't improve. Though trying to help, Cath privately disliked these outings. She wanted to be out with a boy, not her mother.

One evening, Edna asked her to fetch her glasses. Cath entered her mother's now lonely room. Hunting for the glasses, she opened a drawer and saw neatly folded, a pile of Harold's handkerchiefs. The sight of them, no longer needed, brought home his death. Tears began on her way downstairs.

Since the funeral, Edna hadn't cried, at least when the twins were around. After a bout of flu, she looked strange and Cora rang Lulu and Osbert. They arrived to see Edna in bed, her eyes glazed. Lulu exclaimed

'She looks just like last time!'

'God forbid! But you're right.' agreed Osbert. They didn't want to repeat the mental hospital fiasco – their mother had come out much worse. Osbert and his pregnant girl Rita were about to marry, though only Lulu knew. After talking it over, all agreed that the newly married pair should live at 11 Windsor Drive, to look after Edna and the twins.

Fresh from a Registry Office ceremony, Rita joined Osbert at his old home. She wasn't at all what the twins had expected. Far from being some sweet seduced maiden, they suspected she had set up the whole thing herself. Cool, assured, she wore the trousers in more ways than one. She at once delighted and terrified the clones. Though Edna seemed not to improve, a new sense of fun began in the house.

'Let's have some nurks!' Rita would say of an evening. Bert, as she called him, would drive off for steaming fish and chips. In spite of her pregnancy, her energy seemed endless. Not since the days of the char had the house looked so spruce. Sometimes she shouted at the twins
'Couldn't you do something for a change?'
'Well what would you like us to do?' Cath asked. Rita insisted 'It's for you to offer.'
'I don't know about you,' Cath said to Cora 'but with my asthma, I'm exhausted at the thought of it.' Seeing their slowness, Rita ended up doing most of the housework herself. She showed the pair how to make beautiful coffee. With colourful salads and great cakes, meals now became fun. As she put an egg in a slicer for a salad, Cora enthused 'Where did you get that cunning gadget?'
'I bought it. Your mother didn't have a thing. Where's she been all these years?'
'It was Dad.' Cath told her, 'She had to ask for every penny.....'
'I'm sorry for your Mum, but if Burt tried that on, he'd soon get short shrift from me.'

The only thing Rita couldn't take to was Pedro, the poor fox terrier. Mostly house bound during Harold's illness, she now let the dog run wild in the streets. Neighbours complained as he showed a new taste for gay sex, mounting their pets on their walks. The twins' eyes filled when Rita had him put down.

A letter from Bonnie arrived, with news of her recent wedding. Her wartime life had been very hush hush and the family had heard little since. From the letter they learned of amazing events. As secretary to a naval commander, she'd been the only wren serving at sea through the war!

'Good old Bonnie!' said Osbert. Envious, the twins conjured up visions of partying, with glamorous Bonnie the toast of the ship.

A Petty Officer now, Bonnie had often neared an engagement. These had fallen through when she confessed to not wanting children. In déjà vu, she would see the crying twins and relive the trauma of her mother.

'How anyone can want a screaming kid I'll never know!' she had shocked the lovers. She had then met Tim Morrison, an officer on the ship. Since their de-mob, he had landed a job as area manager, covering a fair sized territory. They had married two months ago and now lived in Torquay.

Continually depressed, Edna's friends, even Lilian, deserted her. All that is except one, Ivy Beddows. Dark skinned, she joked about a Spanish grandmother. She spoke little but was loyal, continually visiting, with little reward. As their mother clutched at the twins crying

'My two girls!', they could think of nothing to say. As the months passed, anxiety gave way to despair. Rita and Osbert couldn't cope and Edna was again a 'voluntary' patient.

On Christmas Day, Rita got up early to stuff the turkey. She had it in the oven, bacon and all, well before nine o'clock. Then she began on the breakfast. Osbert and the twins crawled down sleepy eyed, not noticing how she picked at her food. Cora and Cath went up to their room to fetch presents. There was a sweater for Rita, too small now, but they hoped it would fit when her baby was born.

'Thanks Love.' she said, without much enthusiasm, as did Osbert when he opened his tie. The pair opened their presents, identical jumpers, and after sherry and cake, sat down to have a good read. Pleasantly aware of the crackling fire, the smell of the cooking, they didn't miss their mother. Unconsciously, they felt relieved without her sad presence.

Rita had had sherry and a gin and tonic or two, when she set off with Bert for the Spotted Cow. Their regular crowd were all there, waiting for the Colne Valley Beagles. On her return, Rita turned pale as cooking smells wafted through the hall. Osbert stood ready to carve, as she got the great bird from the oven. The twins were trying to help but not sure what to do. As Rita rushed up the long flight of stairs, they whispered

'Is it too much gin?'

'Or the baby?' Aroused at last from his usual lethargy, Osbert roared at the twins.

'Isn't it time you did summat to help? Get these vegetables on the plates, while I finish carving this bird.' They did as he told them, but without Rita, Christmas had lost its sparkle.

Round about five on Boxing Day, the twins made a turkey salad. Rita came down looking better.

'Are we going out for a jar Love?' she asked. Osbert smiled

'Yes Lass.' his evening out now assured. He seldom went anywhere without Rita. His earlier attempts at a night with the lads had resulted in banishment to the dog house (his old attic room). Shouting 'Druffen bugger!', Rita had paced like a lioness through the rooms.

Cath had never made a second visit to the nerve specialist. No one else had remembered it, through the recent chaos. Since her mother had been back in hospital, Cath was determined to stay out of the asylum system herself. She let the appointment stay forgotten. Since Rita's arrival, she had been much happier and felt that she didn't need it.

Curious things were happening at the college. A great influx of displaced persons had swept in. Mainly Polish, they were taking woven textiles, Huddersfield being known for high class suitings. The architects were put out by rivals being after their girls. The Poles worked mainly in the new tech, though some classes were in the art school building. Only one woman, a Hungarian, appeared on the scene. For some months she wore the same clothes in perpetual brown. No one knew why. Then the word got round. Her jacket sweaters and skirts were made from dyed uniforms and blankets!

In the spring, with others from the college, the twins joined a tennis club. They seldom played, their tennis being abysmal. The scent of grasses, the view from a hilly rise, were pleasures enough. As spring greened into summer, they sat at small tables sipping drinks and gazing at the stir of the tree tops. Cath put aside books to listen to the general chatter.

Several members were 'displaced persons', gradually becoming part of the community. Angela and her sultry satellite soon followed, as ever, in search of variety. Joy, having finished with Ellis and his luxury car, was regularly seen with Vic Polanski. A natural blond, he wore the shortest of shorts. His tanned limbs in action were the highlight of play for the girls. As a Catholic, he had seen Joy at church. Before long, the two were engaged. Cath's only brush with the central Europeans was brief. Lingering one evening with a balding Hungarian, kisses and fumblings in the darkening pavilion made her inexperience plain. He disappointingly advised

'Find yourself a young man of eighteen'.

Cora also became briefly involved with a man. At an afternoon matinee at the Theatre Royal, a conversation began with a man. A doctor, he had a practice in a select part of the town. After talking about her work, he invited Cora to look at his collection. The centrepiece was a sketch by Ruskin of an archway in Italy. More unfamiliar were some of sombre caves, woodland slashed by rain and wind. She loved these and was about to ask the artist's name. With scarcely a pause she found herself lying on a rich Iranian rug. A fire, marble framed, threw its warmth on her now nude flesh. His touch, so delicate so unexpected, was impossible to resist.....

The doctor continually phoned, but Cora feared pregnancy. She had been lucky this time. Cath was curious. She proposed

'Suggest a meeting, he'll never know the difference if I turn up instead.' She arranged to meet at the Ritz bar. The deception amused the twins, but it didn't work out. Bored over drinks by a recital of Cath's artistic assumptions, he cut short the evening. He bundled her from the car without even a kiss, at the gate of 11 Windsor Drive.

Some months later Cath met her 'boy of eighteen'. Physically, Basil wasn't all she was looking for. Still she could take his auburn frizz and receding chin. She after all was no beauty. She hardly noticed his limp, caused by childhood polio. Slowed down by her asthma, their pace was in tune. Cath first met Basil at an evening class. Working as a clerk in a stuffy mill office, he envied the full time students. He would go into tirades on their time wasting slackness, loathing his own inopportune background. An only child of divorced parents, he lived on the edge of Huddersfield's biggest council estate. His home was on a main road, opposite the neat gardens and sheltering trees of private houses.

Approaching his home on her first visit, Cath felt low. The scent of flowering cherries faded as she crossed the wide road. Grey concrete under grey clouds, the steep gabled blocks were pierced by entries, stark and prison like as was their plank and wire fencing. Gradually she felt easier as, inside the house, she saw it was neat and clean. More so than her own home before Rita came. She noticed bookshelves, with titles on history politics philosophy.

'Mine.' smiled Basil as Cath looked them over. The ducks in flight on the wall surprised her. She had thought such things part of a thrown away past. Basil's mother was nowhere in sight.

'Dad divorced Mam.' he told Cath, looking away as he spoke. 'While he was in the army my mother was a prostitute more or less. There were men in uniforms here every night – the bloody League of Nations! She works in a garage now – livin' with the owner.'

'My father's dead and my mother's in a mental home.' Cath said, 'That makes us just about quits!' As she finished, his father brought in a salad tea, then tinned pears and cream. As they sat by a window facing the bus stop, Basil and his father lifted their cups in mock invitation at the queue outside. It was easy to pick out those from the private houses. Men in trilbys, women with accessories carefully matched. With younger women it was harder to tell, but the flat caps of the men left little in doubt.

Cora had got religion! It began with a visit to Huddersfield by evangelist Billy Graham. The enormous crowd filled Thorndale Park. Cora and Dot, having nothing particular to do that Sunday, had wandered along. To Dot's amazement, Cora had marched up to be saved in the straggling line of converts. Asked to find a place of worship in her own locality, she had chosen the nearby chapel. With its dome and sober round arched windows, it was a familiar sight though unnoticed. Soon she was a

regular there. The Miss Withers, the headmistress twins, still attended. As always, they had dressed in identical outfits, one navy one green. Pleased to see an ex Thorndale pupil, they asked
'Where's your sister my dear?'

Cath didn't embrace Cora's newly found faith. What enthused her about religions was their art, especially in the East; the Indian Pine, as the misnamed Paisley; from the farther East, the quivering energy of their ball eyed beasts. In their drawings she loved the calm of peaks suspended in voids, with temples and figures infinitely small.

Chapter 9

At College the pace increased in the final year. Cath, her intermediate passed, had caught up with the rest, ready to jump the last hurdle. Under Ted Marshall's sharp eye, they began their designs, to be screen printed later at exam time. With his constant
'Get a move on!', rushing from one to another, he seemed ready for an instant coronary.

Gathering around the break time radiators, they discussed the holidays. Especially the fortnight's fruit picking, which Cath had foregone for Basil. It was 'holidays at home' again for her. Of the five that had gone, only three stayed the course. Just four days after leaving, Cora was on the doorstep blinking back tears. Apparently she had refrained from apple eating at first, unlike most. When she finally gave in, too naive for deceit, she was spotted and sacked on the spot. Another unfortunate victim was Dot. She only lasted one day. Her asthma, dormant for years, had flared up in the heavily scented outdoors. Speechless and half conscious, she was plied with Cora's ephedrine tablets and dragged to a waiting van. The last they saw of her was a wan smile through the steam of an elderly train.

The girls had doubted that Angela was quite as rumoured. They soon found out. Each night exhausted, they fell into sleeping bags after drinks at the pub. From Angela's place unmistakable sounds crescendoed. Later, after a repeat performance, a man would creep out into the dark.
'I couldn't do without it now!' she countered their complaints.

At College, skin and hair deep gold, Angela passed the group at the radiator, busy in their whispered re-telling.
'Don't fight over me boys!' she smiled, as architects grabbed her in passing. Listening, Cath's hopelessness grew. Should she give Basil up? He had proved disappointing. His clumsy lovemaking didn't arouse. Their relationship seemed bleak as the slopes of the Pennines. She felt like some plant on one of its peaks, sunless, battered by storms. Somewhere there was richness and joy. Would it always elude her?

Rita's baby Graham was the centre of attention at 11 Windsor Drive. The twins had little time to help, spending most evenings in homework or at classes. Not many cinema visits now. At college they hardly noticed the new intake of first-years, with the exception of one who could scarcely be missed. Small, blond pony tail flying, Jenny missed nothing of what was going on, in or out of the college. She made a strong pass at Joy's fiancee, the honey haired Vic, but without success. She had a multitude of clothes and more shoes than anyone had seen since the war. Rumours spread of black market dealings, clothing coupons still being around.

The staff were working flat out for the finals. Ted Marshall, ignoring the theorists, transformed students' efforts. A hairy hand, with a touch here, a touch there, brought dreary daubs to life, enthusing students. With ideas of working as a freelance along with his teaching, he got out a collection of fabric designs. They seemed brilliant to the students, but he came back depressed from his trip to the textile barons of Manchester. He hadn't sold a single one.

'To hell with it,' he thought, 'I've got a job here, they can do what they like over there.' His visit had opened a small world. Long flights of stairs and the odd clattering lift had led to innumerable attic rooms. Here under sky lit windows, bowed figures bent over work, not daring to raise an elbow. On Cambridge Road at the Calico Printing Federation, neat suited men sneered at his work. Europeans continually tried new methods. Here the clanging steam age wheels still rolled out prints, near as dated as the machines themselves.

Eric Crowther too, in his casual way, was pushing the students. Though he never altered their drawings, he often drew a how to do it piece in a corner. Overwrought as exams neared, he got laryngitis and could scarcely speak.

'No need for you to whisper too Miss Hunt!' he croaked among laughs, as Cath unconsciously copied him. Cath's life drawing was improving, though still behind her sister's. Staff rated Cora's work among the best ever seen in the school.

Rita's brother Andrew, for some years senior chemist with one of the large groups, had bought a chemist shop. Modernisation being needed, he had asked Osbert to be plumber and electrician, an opportunity Rita thought not to be missed. Osbert was not so sure. For weeks he dithered. He'd have to take on more men and get finance. He finally decided against it. Rita was furious

'I thought you'd got money when I married you!' she shouted.

'And I thought you'd got money!' Bert returned, as she went on

'I know your property's not much, but it's security to borrow on. Now you've an opportunity and you won't take it! It'll be man and boy for the rest of our lives.' Bert said no more. He knew she was right, but though dead, his father had sapped his confidence for good.

Cora had taken up ballroom dancing and acquired a remarkable boyfriend. Morris was a misfit. On his psychiatrist's advice he had left his parents and lived in a bedsit. Here books surrounded him, many bound by himself, at his bookbinding job, also arranged by his psychiatrist. His bizarre behaviour was worst on the dance floor. He would whirl the frail Cora around in a rhythm entirely his own. A member of the young communist league at almost thirty, conversion was one of his aims. He soon persuaded Basil. The twins and their paramours had many an argument, washed down by bitter or mild. Cath would gaze longingly at the rosy lounge bar with its comfortable seats, but it was spit and sawdust or nothing. One evening Rita stood at the door with Osbert as the quartet set off for the pub. She laughed

'The twins have some bloody funny boy friends don't they?'

'But look at the twins!' answered Osbert.

At college, as Jenny sauntered around with expensive Joyce shoes and Jacqmar scarves, Ted thought of head scarf designs. Novelty ones would be great for the girls. They set to work with enthusiasm. Cath had what seemed a brilliant idea, a park seen through elegant railings. Discouraged as they were from using a reference, it wasn't quite as she'd hoped. Joy turned out design after brilliant design, or so it seemed to Cath.

Another suggestion Ted had thrown out was little croquets for dress fabrics. Since his abortive visit to the cotton metropolis these hadn't been mentioned. Cath tried some and found they came easily. They were small and speedy and she could get more done in the time. She got a collection together. Ted was impressed. He advised her to apply for Royal College, along with the illustrator Jim Walton. Accepted for the exam, they were closeted in a room together. Jim began right away on some great looking work. As Cath pored over the papers, a paralysis set in. Nothing seemed remotely relevant. She decided to tackle the head scarf, launching into a classical theme. In a panic she began on a border of figures. The time seemed incredibly short. As the colours stared back at her heavy and dull, panic turned to despair. Ted's face, as he gathered up the papers, said it all.

Surprisingly Jim also failed the exam. He created a diversion with his book 'Addled Art'. It rocketed around among the students. A visit to the touring Picasso exhibition had caused a furore among them. Many of the paintings looked tatty to Cora. A stuck on ticket was peeling off. Cath saw the excitement of the show. Though bursting with 'significant form', the colourful work was hard to fathom. 'Woman in a Fish Hat', what could it mean? Still, that the master's work had come to their town was thrilling enough.

Jim's book, a rubbishing of established moderns, reinforced the majority view. They turned on Cath, though mainly in fun.
'Is this the trash you've been pouring over in all those books?'.
'When you could have been out with a boy!'
The comments were endless. She suffered a 'crisis of faith'. Had all her burrowing through art books been in vain? She leafed through the dramatic scenes of John Piper. They still looked richly authentic. Less so was Graham Sutherland's 'Gordale Scar'. A mess of splashes in varying greens, it bore no relation to the scene of its name. She put away the books and channelled her thoughts into possible jobs.

Another diversion came some weeks later. The displaced persons from wool and textiles, were having their finals. Staff had heard that cheating was common in Europe, so they moved the exams to the art school building. The examinees were more or less frisked after toilet stops. A huge queue formed, chattering and grabbing at passing girls. Joy forsook the radiators for chats with Vic, while Angela and her friend made hay.

Poor Edna was now home, with no apparent change. Her fragile contact with family broken, her isolation had deepened. The twins got her library books. Rita talked to her.

'Come on Lass! Let's have a smile!' Edna couldn't respond. Her mind wandered from the books. Images intruded, a chair, a barred window, tendrils of ivy curling outside. How she had envied that ivy. Outside at last, she found she just wanted to die. When everyone was out, she searched the twins' bedroom and found ephedrine tablets. She'd got half of them down, when the nausea began. She fought with it, trying to keep the drug down, but she dashed to the sink just in time and spewed them all back. She told no one. Having to drag her from bed every morning, Bert sought the Doctor's advice. He sent in an ex district nurse as keeper, watching her every move. Dour and unimaginative, the woman provided no stimulus for their mother. Though the family felt guilty, there seemed little else they could do.

'Let's buy the lass some new clothes,' Rita said one evening and the twins agreed. On Saturday they took her round town. It wasn't a success. Edna turned a glazed eye over coats suits and dresses, but nothing sparked interest Cora whispered to Cath

'D' you remember how keen Mum was, always mixing and matching her colours?' Cath agreed

'She knew what was in and what was out, though Dad put her off what she'd chosen.'

'What about this Love?' Rita asked and Cora suggested

'Isn't this what you like?' Still Edna said nothing, staring anywhere but at the clothes. In the end, Rita chose her an outfit and they ended the unfortunate spree.

The final exams at the college were now close. Cora's design, to be printed on cream, was a leaf pattern in shades of red-brown. Based on small privet-shaped leaves, it was simple and well drawn, as was all her work. Cath's was much bolder, large sprays of pink flowers, with olive leaves and some touches of black. She printed it on parachute nylon. Cora made an evening dress from hers, long sleeved and elegant, though she had little occasion to wear it. Cath put hers away in a drawer. Parachute nylon was out.

The exam over, there came the worst part, the long wait for results. Fortunately all had passed. Everyone was full of their plans. Dot landed a design job with the Calico Printing Federation in Manchester, rather to the staff's surprise. They hadn't noticed the strides made in the work of 'Hop along Cassidy', always quietly persistent. Jim Walton had taken a local job, designing mugs for the coming coronation. He didn't foresee its short life. The Royal event over, he was given his cards. Cath had failed to get into Royal College. A door had opened onto a bright world, the capital's glitter, galleries, theatres...... That door closed abruptly.

Cora and she were to spend the next year on a teaching course in Leeds. Neither of them wanted to teach. Bert and Rita had sought the advice of Veronica Owen, their Grammar School teacher. She had suggested the move. She was sure the commercial world wouldn't suit the twins, and Osbert agreed. Rita couldn't see them as teachers, but felt they should have the chance. It was what their father had wanted.

Joy, soon to marry, was starting a job as a tracer locally, Vic now designing at one of the town's mills. Dot had started her prestigious job, designing furnishings in the cotton capital. Angela, the 'tart of the town', had screwed back her waves into a doughnut bun for an interview. To the architects' amusement she got the job, teaching art at a select private school!

Joy invited the twins to her wedding. St. Cuthberts Catholic church had a huge congregation. For the wedding the crowd flowed into the churchyard. Cora and Cath found a seat some rows back. The genuflecting, the bobbing up and down confused them, as they tried to copy parishioners. Some sniggered at their ill timed efforts. Cora was hardly aware of this, absorbed by the glowing candles, the swinging censer. The sonorous Latin swept her into a fervour, unknown in the familiar chapel. Joy passed down the aisle her face rapt at the sight of Vic, haloed by a burst of sun.

Chapter 10

Cath glanced along their pine floored hall with its tasselled Spanish rug. Her husband had spent hours laying it. From the opened outer doorway the green of leaves filtered through the coloured glass of the inner door. Sea greens, blues and purples shed their radiance on white walls. Cath had created the art nouveau panel some ten years earlier, in the seventies. She had intended to recreate an enchantment sensed in childhood, when lamp lit rooms had jewelled windows, lighting winter snows or summer evening trees. These rooms enfolded guests. Their massive outer doors shut out those such as she, gazing along gated drives.

Deep in reverie, Cath was hardly aware of covering the distance, as she approached the local station. With sudden excitement she caught sight of Kent, from the building society in Hexham. She began a tentative 'Hello' but saw he had no eyes for her. His smile, so reminiscent of the tenant of Shandy Hall, was for a woman stepping from the train. Alert, eager, placing an arm caressingly about her shoulders, he swept her onto the platform. Entering the train Cath watched through the grimy glass as they disappeared.

'Well, good luck to them...' she thought. She was curious about the contrast between his excitable air at times and the forlorn abstracted gaze she had noticed. He had had this expression when he called at her house one evening, to offer her new work. As she let him in, lamp lit hues played over his features, instantly transformed to their excited state. He swept an appreciative glance around the scene. Flashing a smile, he asked 'Remember me?' She knew what she wanted to say, but couldn't find words. Rushing to collect the work, in her confusion, she had hardly let him set foot in the hall, before she was closing both doors. Whatever the rapport, she couldn't encourage it. There was no way she wanted another divorce. It was probably pure fantasy in any case.

Cath recalled another evening when she and Kent had each attended the same baroque concert. She was unaware that he had been there, until he sat beside her on the train back to Hexham. His talk had enlivened their journey, but she was glad now, that she hadn't let him walk with her to her door as he had offered. Today, though disappointed at Kent's obvious delight in his station companion, in some sense she now felt relieved. In any case, it was years since she had seen him. She recalled her destination. Soon she may be unable to see him, or anyone, clearly again.

She left the crowded station and was on her way to hospital for laser treatment to her right eye. It was now showing signs of the same deterioration as in the left. She hoped that good right vision would last until she'd produced some editions of prints in her series.

Outpatients gave her directions to 'Pavilion 2'. The name conjured visions of shore temples, their steps brilliant with saris. Bright wings soared over fringing palms..... She felt almost lost among endless corridors. They were overheated and heavy with strange smells. She peered at high up signs, scarcely able to see them. Then sighting 'Pavilion 1', she knew she was almost there. The young doctor explained that laser treatment would be painless. When Cath asked what was the cause of her problem, all she got was

'That's the sort of question you shouldn't ask'. Thoughts of sexually transmitted diseases flashed through her mind, though her GP had said there was nothing of that sort in her records. The laser treatment was just a dull thud and a blaze of primaries.

On her exit, Cath decided to call at the Hanover Press to arrange for the printing of her plates. Her worsening vision put her off messing with acids and inks. Stepping into harsh sunlight, she put on dark glasses. Curious, she watched the phenomenon that moved as she focused. It looked like a piece of delicate black lace or a coppice of winter trees. Actually it was the remains of blood vessels, cauterised to prevent the eye damage spreading. Though the branch effect would go, she assumed the result would be permanent.

'Hi Cath!' called Sheena Rama, at the press. She looked all in, attempting to mix ink with son Shiva perched on her arm. She had given up teaching, but was doing new work. Her dark hair, tied on top with a scarf, flopped around in lank pieces. The white make-up with bright lipstick, deep shadow, called up an image of a melancholy Pierrot. Other unknown girls, with the same clown faces, floated around, plus a couple of spiky haired youths. Nearly all wore black. Goths Cath had heard they were called. Cath felt her old green jeans and green bordered lemon tee shirt were inappropriate, but she wasn't about to buy any all-black gear.

She glanced at one girl's etching plate, assuming it to be an abstraction, until it startlingly coalesced into a penis. Casting her eye next on a proof of Sheena's latest work, Cath saw a change from her earlier prints, on Hindu temples and dance. The style was much freer, dark and indistinct. She could see a thrashing figure on its back, while another hurled around what appeared to be the other's entrails. These guts exploded into street scenes, old and new. Assuming the theme to be Hindu, Cath asked

'A scene from the 'Ramayana'?' Sheena answered

'No, I'm not into that now. It's the two Rippers – Jack and the Yorkshire one.'

Now that Cath came to think about it, it figured. Sheena came from Yorkshire, from the mining village where Cath and Cora had camped with the Guides.

Cath found an unusually clean chair and began work on her latest print. She hadn't been to the press for some time, having landed a commission for some greeting cards. Now, via the buzzing voices, she hoped to hear of recent happenings there. Max Vernon drifted in occasionally, to do the lithographic part of his work. He was part of the art establishment these days. He sold whole editions to London galleries, as fast as he could complete them.

Cath had noticed, in the showcase for finished work, a signed print by Roy Clement. Since getting an agent, he had had some success in illustration work. She was surprised at seeing his signature on this piece, a view of a classical church near the Newcastle quayside. Drawn in a loose bold style, it was very different from his previous meticulous work. She pieced together from snippets of conversation, that he had recently been near to a breakdown. He had worked flat out for over a year.

Requests for alterations by finicky editors had meant that he was scarcely able to manage. The art world was far from a picnic, she thought. Little of the money was made by the artist, whichever way you looked at it.

Cath asked about editioning her prints and found that a lot had changed at the press. Assistance from North East Arts had solved the press's monetary problems. Mike Pattinson, a high flier fresh from Royal College had arrived as a director, teaching litho and screen. He would be doing Cath's editioning. An admin director, in the new plush showroom, sold prints and put on exhibitions. Photography and plate making were farmed out to Free Print, a new co-operative in the building. A notice appeared in a nearby printers, eaking out a living with letterpress equipment. It read pathetically, in a dated type, 'This is not Free Print' Another printer had been about to give Cath some freelance work. Showing some graphics, she told him

'I had these printed at Free Print.' His face took on a closed expression and the work wasn't forthcoming.

Cath hung around in the screen workshop, while Mike, tall blond, finished dealing with a visitor. He was explaining to the awkward customer that they no longer did commercial work such as posters. Convinced at last, the man went out.

'Could this caption be screen printed onto the plate?' Cath asked.

'No problem' said Mike, 'I'll get it printed at Free Print for you. OK?'

'Fine.' Cath nodded, 'Whenever you can manage it.' Leaving plate and caption with him she walked out.

She passed the screens where Stan Polanski was working, in his fast haphazard manner. Greying, chunky, she guessed him to be about her own age. As he placed work on a drying stand, she saw he had printed only two colours. All she knew about him was that he was Polish, an asylum seeker in World War Two. His early prints were lino-cuts; sharply contrasted in white and heavy black. They showed groups of figures under arches, or on starkly lit roads. In others, figures were dwarfed by factories or vast blocks of flats. His screen prints were very different. There was drawing and collage, scraps of newspaper, odd shapes cut from black or crepe paper. Added were energetic brush strokes, letters and numbers. All the work had a nightmare quality, the more powerful for being less than explicit. Cath wanted to know more of Stan's past.

At the press Christmas party, she had tried to make conversation with him and his wife. They were the only people of similar age there.

'Your work's great,' she had said to him, 'but what's it about?'

'I'll let you have a look through my folder later, if you like.' he had suggested. Cath agreed. The Goths were there, though not Sheena. Dressed in blood red, black or funeral purple, most had black lipstick and Egyptian style eyes. Like a bunch of Morticias, they stood around drinking and discussing the Shelleys and their ilk.

'I've started something really Byronic.' said one, to her lank haired partner.

'Have you now.' he countered, waving black fingernails.

'I'll have to come up and see that some time...'

After too much wine, Cath was seeing two Goths where one had been before. As she left through one door, Stan came through another, portfolio in hand. By now she was incapable of looking at his work. She didn't have the bottle to ask to see it another time. She never did get to see his work.

As she started for home, it was dark and chilly in the square. The lit-up signs of the F.E.P.O.W. Club and the Chinese restaurants added a cheer to the scene. Their scents of aniseed and unknown spices wafted from doorways, giving way to vinegar and chips. Through a window, she glanced sympathetically at a youth, wiping an already spotless white counter. Blue florescent tubes chilled the scene, in spite of red tablecloths. The sign, in stubby plastic letters, announcing
   'FISH AND CHIPS
   POT OF TEA
   BREAD AND BUTTER
   SIT DOWN'
hadn't drawn anyone in. The place had only just opened, in premises

abandoned for some time, but it already seemed doomed. She could be wrong. It was only four thirty. Crowds might turn up in an hour. The prospects for its next door neighbour didn't look too hopeful either. For years she had seen the same traditional leather suite in its window. Though no doubt dusted, fluff was gathering round its buttons. There were few sounds. Just the odd car, getting away from city centre traffic. Next to some sleazy toilets, a brightly lit shop was doing well. Student types were trying on its second hand clothes, some spilling out on the pavement.

'Look at this Kiddo, just right for tonight!' and

'What about this?' broke the quiet.

Cath put up her hood, as a light rain began falling.

In adjoining streets, impressive new Chinese restaurants had replaced small firms, struggling in old properties. One in particular attracted Cath. Its doorway of jade coloured tiles supporting a mock roof looked worthy of the Forbidden City itself. Patterned disks capped its tubular tiles, reminiscent of ancient wooden structures. The eaves curved as if to some opiate heaven. Along wet pavements, brilliant signs were twinned.

Part 3

Chapter 11

Wearing their new suits, the twins spent a morning in Huddersfield. Their jackets had the new flared 'peplums', Cath's in beige and Cora's in a startling flame. Cath preferred Cora's but now they dressed differently. They had also splashed out on summer straw hats, Cora's in beige and Cath's in dark brown. Although hats were in, the twins weren't used to them and felt ridiculous. It didn't help that they overheard Rita saying to Bert

'They look like a couple of early Victorians don't they?'

In Field's cafe they saw several faces they knew. Angela was there among a laughing crowd. Nearby were Victor and Joy, chatting with another just married couple. Hat stands nodded over dark oak panels half hiding the intimate groups around tables. Under a potted palm were Edna's old friends, former friends as they now were. The twins had looked forward to marzipan fruits, again available, but they said little as they swallowed their cakes. Each thought of her mother, reminded by seeing the friends. Would she ever be free of that prison, or would she serve a life sentence?

On the following day, the twins took a train to Leeds. They were continuing their teaching course at Leeds College of Art. From the train, the twins saw suburbs. Houses with gardens and trees appeared and the green of parks within crescents and terraces. As they neared the city centre, the train passed streets of commercial buildings. Sturdily classical, gothic or with hints of the East, they stretched to where back-to-back houses began. These crowded in bleak streets around the brick mills, with signs reading 'Mungo, Shoddy and Rags'. Pubs and chapels were common. Church steeples pierced the smoke. Mile after mile of these streets stretched away, the gable ends to the railway. Outside the Station entrance the girls could see City Square, Titty Square as it was known on account of its topless statues. Their over fleshed forms contrasting oddly with the delicate stems of their lily lamps.

The art college was close to the main station. There were tempting cafes in little side streets, where the twins occasionally ate. It was a relief from their teaching attempts. They taught alternate days at a Huddersfield secondary school and a Leeds primary school. They were reassured to find that they knew the art teacher at the secondary school, Mrs Forbes, from their time in the guides. She had passed them for their child nurse badges. She was kind but her advice wasn't easy to follow. In Cora's first class, she was scared her arrangement for still life was too small. An assortment of jewellery on heavily draped velvet, its brilliance was lost to those further back. They were out to get fun from the student. Girls giggled, whispering

'Look at her skinny legs!'

'She looks terrified!' said another. Boys tried to shock with muttered obscenities.

'.....tossing off!' caught her ear, but she ignored it. The rowdiness grew and finally the headmaster called Cora into his room.

'If things don't improve,' he told her, 'another school will have to be found for you.'

Worse even than the secondary school, was Kirkstone Road, a primary school near the centre of Leeds. In blackened brick, it stood next to the grounds of the old Kirkstone Abbey. A twelfth century ruin, its few stunted trees were the only ones in sight. At each session, as Cath reluctantly neared the school, panic gripped her, but she forced herself on. Passing the hall, she saw little change from her own pre war school. Feet clad in pumps, thudded on the floor boards, to the same depressing old tunes.

'If all the world were paper and all the seas were ink' was the one she really detested. It conjured up white trees and oceans of the blue black ink, still in the ink wells of the old brown desks.

A singularly embarrassing day was the one on which staff had pinned Cath's work on the classroom walls. Intended to be talked through, the work was well beyond her reach. While she looked around vaguely, a small girl brought her a chair. To jeers from thirty small mouths, she crimsoned and mounted the chair, all discipline lost. The twins had hoped they would improve as the term progressed, but instead they got worse. They felt trapped and began to plan their escape.

Autumn was an Indian summer that year. Unable to afford one of the new billowing underskirts, Cath had made herself one. She used some old bed linen, edged with hand crocheted lace by her grandmother. Rita was about to throw it out. Just as Cath hoped, the stiffly starched petticoat made her skirt stand out from diminutive hips. A half-inch of lace peeped below. She was braless at Basil's request. They took a bus going south. It jolted to a halt, near a signpost marked Netherdene.

'This looks fine!' enthused Basil, limping down the steps, Cath following. Near woods, falling leaves speckled the calm of the fields. Cath was on an ephedrine high. Under a hazy sun they made love among the whiteness of her linen. As they followed the footpath to Netherdene village, elder flowers had an illusory glow.

By the time they saw the slate roofs of cottages, Basil was limping badly. Cath was breathless with asthma and needed more ephedrine. Resting on a bank they downed their packed food. As they crested a hill, Netherdene spread out below. Small street of terraces thinned out to cottages and farms. On the main road were shops, including a little antique shop. In the centre of the window was a collection of jewellery. Cath remarked of an opal ring

'That ring has lovely sea colours.' They glanced cursorily at the glassware and pottery.

'More junk than antique.' they decided. They passed on to explore the streets and alleyways.

'You liked that ring didn't you?' Basil asked unexpectedly,

'Why don't we get engaged?' Cath's reactions were mixed. She had enjoyed the day. Sex had been surprisingly good but would it last? At least they had interests in common. She agreed. Returning to the shop, Basil bought the ring, putting it on Cath's finger right away. Cath mused

'We'll never have much money, but maybe a little cottage like the ones around here......'   His father wouldn't be pleased, Basil knew.

'Yond lass 'll not make you a wife.' he had warned, 'She'll be no good at housework with her asthma. You'd best look elsewhere.'

'It's my business!' Basil countered. Her reading and music mattered more to him. What healthy woman would look at him anyway?

Finishing their food on the bus, the couple returned to 11 Windsor Drive to baby sit. In the kitchen with Rita, Cath showed her the ring.

'Opals for tears Love.' grinned her sister-in-law. Seeing the hard little face stiffen, she gave her a warning glance.

'You don't love him do you?' was all she had to say. Cath said nothing, but she knew Rita was right.

The twins and their boyfriends shivered as they drank their cold beer in the pub's unheated tap room. At first the two couples had little to say. They soon reached the stage, new to the twins, of unawareness of neighbouring drinkers. It was a revelation to Cath, to speak without fear of looking a fool!

'How's the cycling club,' Basil asked Morris.

'Oh I've given it up for the winter,' he replied.

'In actual fact it might be for good. My psychiatrist advises against it.' Heads turned, but Morris, unembarrassed, spoke louder.

'Dr. Izacs told me I'd joined the club to cycle away from my problems.' he went on. Cath laughed

'That's ridiculous! I'd be on a bike tomorrow if I could forget the pollen.'

'And if you could cycle!' added Cora.

'By the way, about the Party,' Morris went on. 'The YCL are looking for new members.'

He had tried his Young Communist line on Cora without success. Her faith was now veering from Chapel to High Church. Sundays now saw her in St Michael of All Angels, where incense scented the aisles.

Basil and Cath were more likely converts. Disappointment had soured Basil. From his evening class in advertising he had hoped for a break. Remarks such as

'We're not a charitable institution!' greeted him on his studio trail. He fumed about the college full timers,

'Cracking their time wasting gags, I'd show them what work was if I had the chance.'

'Most ads are a laugh.' Cath countered, 'A bit of a laugh might get you results.'

'That lot 'll get their deserts!' Basil had forecast, slumping into one of his moods. Morris fed the couple with pamphlets. Cath was naively impressed. Pouring over copies of 'Soviet Union', the flag waving crowds seemed the answer to her own isolation. The Young Communist League gained two new members.

It became obvious that the twins weren't cut out for teaching. Even so, Cora wished to carry on, in spite of her worsening asthma. Cath wanted to draw out the inhibited loners, but with so little joy of her own felt powerless. Finally she wrote to the Calico Printing Federation, though all the best jobs would be taken by then. Hearing nothing, she decided on a treck round the studios doing work for the Fed. The nightmare trail led up endless stairways in liftless buildings. Most studios didn't even look at her portfolio.

'We don't want a-a-rt students. We train our own people straight from school.' sneered one manager, voicing the common view. Jobless and practically collapsing from asthma, Cath caught a return train. She felt that her years at college were a waste. If she couldn't teach and wasn't wanted here, what on earth else could she do?

However a week later, both twins were interviewed and given jobs in the Federation's own studios. They had positions in different departments, to start in a month's time. They had turned their backs on teaching and sampled the attitudes of the textile world to college courses. In disgust, the twins never collected their once cherished National Diplomas, left at Leeds college, much to Cath's later regret.

Cora and Cath hated the pall of gloom around their mother and her keeper, always upstairs in her room. The doctor had hinted that their mother was certifiable and the family set up a conference. Lulu and Larry had arrived and joined the twins in front of the fire, with its turquoise tiles in their classic surround. Lulu saw change in the room. A new five lamp fitting hung from the ceiling rose. The near antique sideboard, denuded of ornaments, now sported merely a fruit bowl.

'What are we going to do about Gran then?' asked Rita, broaching the subject directly.

'The doctor said she should go in a mental home for good, unless you've got any ideas.'

'Well you've done your share, I admit.' said Lulu rather reluctantly. 'It's our turn now. We'll try giving her a home.'

'I wouldn't put my mother in one of those places,' Larry broke in, 'Lulu's mum is only depressed after all. At any rate, we'll take her and see how it goes.'

Only depressed! thought Rita, but merely announced brightly 'It's all settled then,' as she served up coffee and snacks.

Freed of her keeper, Edna moved to her daughter's new home. Their family now growing, Lulu and Larry had vacated their flat and were buying a newly built house. First Lulu bought her mother smart clothes. Though Edna wasn't capable of choosing her own, she felt a new woman when she tried them on. From this new self image a transformation began. With the faithful Ivy Bedoes, she ventured to Field's cafe and joined the old crowd. Wakened at seven by her own alarm, she got up right away, before the old brooding took hold. She smiled now and chattered. The twins hardly knew her when they came round. Cora asked Cath

'Why couldn't we work this miracle at home?'

'To my mind, it's company and the getting out.' Cath answered. 'Being shut up with that woman was useless. Some doctor's idea I suppose. They ought to try some of their own medicine, see how they like it!'

Cora and Cath moved to Manchester to start work at the CPF. Cora's work was mainly setting to repeat designs bought in France. Alone with an elderly man, though she liked the challenge of the work, she envied Cath the friendliness of the girls in her studio. Cath on the other hand would have liked to learn setting to repeat. This entailed adding an area around a design in the exact style of the designer and paid well. Cath instead, was a colourist, the lowest of skills in the business and consigned to women. She resented this and couldn't see its creativity.

Six colourways were done to each design. Weaned on the subtle colours in vogue for up-market fashions, Cath detested the sweet pastel shades.

'You hold your brush like the Chinese!' the designer Reynolds remarked irritably, sleeking back what was left of his hair. With strong yet flexible fingers he showed her how to copy the original's single stroke petals.

She didn't mention her asthma, though this caused her problems. On arrival through the rush hour traffic, then mounting the steep stairs, just breathing was so hard. Head and chest bursting, she longed to sit motionless, but must make a start. She rested her elbow on the desk to steady her hand while she drew.

'She doesn't seem to know much, to say she's replacing Joan.' whispered one girl.

'They don't appear to learn much at art school' another hinted, 'I'm glad I didn't waste any time there.' Cath began to realise she had replaced the head colourist and began to feel, as did Reynolds, that she wasn't up to the job.

Cora and Cath stayed at the Y.W.C.A. while they inspected an abysmal series of digs from a list supplied by the company. They trailed up the worn steps of one broken down terrace after another, to view near identical rooms. Each had the same peeling walls, stained carpet, sleazy bed. Disgusted, they finally got lodgings from a newspaper ad, in a leafy street of semis.

The landlady, Doris Swinburn was an oddity. As she had a cleft palette and was deaf, conversation was difficult. It mostly consisted of a rambling monologue on her part. As she seemed to expect little else, the twins got away with the odd yes and no. She doted on her Pekinese dog, Ping Pong, calling it one day Ping next day Pong, or so the twins thought, until they realised there were two. They sympathised with the identical creatures, suffering like them from asthma, due to their flattened noses. The pekes weren't the only objects in the house of Chinese origin. Flanking the fireplace were tall vases with tail chasing dragons. Flat featured animals stared from every shelf.

Poring over art books, Cath had become aware of an intensified face, endlessly recurring in Eastern arts. In human, animal or monstrous forms, it hinted at drug-induced origins. Called 'stylised' in books, it mocked that cool classification. Its terrifying aspect snarled from temple gates in India. The early Americas knew it. Cath had read that the Chinese had bred the flat Pekinese face to resemble their ritualistic beasts. Fish too were tortuously inbred, to mimic the beasts' frenzied glare.

Cora was finished at the C.P.F. almost before she had started! Their new G.P. booked the twins into an asthma clinic for two sessions a week. Cath refused to have time off, but Cora accepted. The company fired her for failing her medical. Cath stayed on alone at the house of the Pekinese. Cora, not showing much regret, was taken in by Lulu. She found work tracing in a Huddersfield drawing office. The twins saw less and less of each other.

Cath gradually bettered her colouring skills. The designs were mostly floral, with a few geometrics and the tedious but mysterious paisley. Dot Carter, now a designer of original furnishings, worked in another department. When they first arrived, she had invited the twins into her studio. She produced up-market florals, taking about three months on each design, including colourways.

'Why don't we go out for a meal sometime?' Dot had asked, but Cath had declined. Dot's company was a constant reminder of her own lack of success.

Cath still spent some weekends at 11 Windsor Drive and some at her digs in Manchester. When Basil had scraped together some money, he would come over. They would take a bus to some stately home. It was raining one Sunday at Windsor Drive.

'Shall I sketch your portrait Basil? Would you like that?' Cath asked. Basil was thrilled as she sat among the settee's cushions with her sketch pad.

'That's brilliant!' he said, gazing at the finished profile of him, huddled over a book.

Coming closer, he fumbled with her breasts. His clumsy touch didn't excite her.

'There must be more to sex than this' she thought, 'I must find someone else, but where?'

'Let's get married and have babies Cath. Let's make it this Summer please.'

'I'll think about it Basil.' she said, getting up, 'Bert and Rita are due back any minute.'

Basil had found work with an advertising agency, starting on the lowest rung with lettering on postcards. It was miserably paid and Cath hesitated to give up her job for marriage. On bus journeys or city streets, she would often see men of real appeal. An expressive mouth, the glance of an eye, would suggest unknown pleasures, but how to reach out and grasp them? She couldn't bring herself to stand in a dance hall crowd, like cattle in a mart.

Influenced by talk at work of the Halle orchestra, Cath listened to the third programme on her ancient radio. She paid a tentative visit to a music club and was welcomed by a slim young woman, expensively dressed. They listened to Walton's Belshazzar's Feast. Everyone around her seemed enthralled. Some were even in tears. Later during coffee, the slim woman said to Cath

'This is my husband.'

She gestured towards a figure filling two of a small row of chairs. Cath gasped! They seemed so ill matched! The creature, enormous and totally bald, glanced up at Cath. His pale lips and heavily lidded eyes expressed a subtle but extreme sensuality quite foreign to Cath. Too embarrassed to look the woman in the eye, she made an excuse and left, trying to weigh up the situation. An arranged marriage? Perhaps there was a synagogue in the area? She didn't return to the club.

At lunch times Cath often strolled past the CPF building down Oxford Street, looking at book shops. Perhaps, as a treat, she would buy a peach from a barrow. At other times, she took a bus to Market Street, where large department stores crowded each other. With little to spend she window shopped, and ate her lunch in Piccadilly Gardens. As she ate she would glance at the buildings around. Lewis's store, smoke blackened, Victorian offices, fronting the park and stretching away. There was an air of decay about some, their filthy windows like eyeless sockets.

Cath's favourite place was a new public library. Circular, the library itself was in the outer part. In the centre was a theatre, plus a snack bar in the basement. Cath was lonely in her lodgings without Cora. Often she would have a snack in the basement, before changing her books. Sometimes she read for over an hour in the deep comfort of an armchair. The decor's simplicity was new and in sharp contrast to the exterior, with its classical portico. Here, she was cocooned from her painful past.

One Saturday, Cora paid a visit. She looked hollow eyed and fragile, though wearing an expensive new dress. On it terracotta flowers trailed over a trellis of sage, echoing the green in a pair of tiny new shoes. In her case were several more pairs, all in exciting shades. Size one and a half, they were window dressing samples now being sold off. Cath was envious, her size being three. Fear swamped the envy, as she looked at her sister. Perhaps Mrs Smithson was right when she whispered

'That girl's not long for this world.'

Cora had heard and they'd laughed. Doctors had said you didn't die of asthma, but Cath wasn't so sure, as they set off for the theatre.

Joan Littlewood's' company was putting on a Commedia del Arte piece and a play by Garcia Lorca. Scenery was a black curtain, in its centre a design of a strange brilliance. This flashed between the players, their clothes picked out in the same bright tones. The show was so new and exhilarating, after the dreary privations of the war. Cath felt she must find a more meaningful life.

Christmas was looming and partying in the studio was a bottle of wine drunk in cups. Reynolds stumbled in with a bottle and a box of cream cakes. His florid face suggested more drink.

'Going anywhere for Christmas?' Cath asked some drinks later.

'Kerbstone Edge that's all!' a girl answered.
'But Christmas at home's the best.' said another.
'If you've got a home!' Cath added, recalling she was spending the holiday at Lulu's.
'God, look at the time! I'll miss my train!' she exclaimed, startled from her wine induced languor. As she struggled into her coat, Reynolds offered
'Come on! We'll get a taxi.'
'I wouldn't go.... one of the girls whispered', but Cath grabbed her battered case and ran with him.

Enclosed behind glass in an old style cab, Reynolds thrust a red cheek against Cath's. Pawing her breasts he began
'You live in Huddersfield where the girls like their udders feeled.....'
Repulsed by words and touch, Cath cringed away.
'How about a weekend with me? No one would ever know...' he went on. Furious but scared for her job, she merely said
'Thanks but no thanks!', as the taxi slowed to a halt. Jumping onto the train, she wished she'd refused the lift and caught the next train. How could she face him next week?

Chapter 12

Post holiday, things were difficult for Cath at the studio. Reynolds came creeping around her. His fleshy face at her cheek he would murmur 'Deepen that red a little more Cath.' If she raised her arm while working, a cupping hand would sneak through. Disgust choked her as his hot penis pressed her thigh. What would the girls think? She couldn't bring herself to mention it and neither did they, but she was sure they had noticed. It was all too embarrassing.

Her thoughts began to turn towards marriage. Basil at least, though not madly desirable, wasn't actually repulsive. The marriage was arranged in June, at St. Michael of All Angels in Huddersfield. Cath handed in her notice at the CPF, with little thought of where they would live, or how they would manage on Basil's minuscule wage.

The honeymooner's left the smoke dark streets behind. Train windows framed rushing fields, lime as the sun broke through. At Whitby the couple struggled off, Cath's asthma worsening.

'Couldn't we get a taxi?' Cath wanted to ask, but knew better.

Basil would collapse on the kerb before he would pay for a taxi and she had little cash. Fortunately, the bus stopped just outside their digs, where an evening meal was ready. As Cath picked at the reheated roast beef and cabbage smothered in a tasteless gravy, she began to worry about cooking for Basil. She would have to buy a book of some kind that was certain. She had never cooked a full meal in her life. Beans or sardines on toast were as much as she'd managed so far.

Cath felt adequately dressed for a change, in her pale blue suit with its matching beret. Tan shoes, bag and sweater completed the outfit. She had also worn the suit for the wedding, with tight navy shoes and a feathery hat. Basil had wanted the Registry Office, but Cath felt its bleakness would be a bad start. Glancing round the ill-furnished room she recalled the church service. Their earlier practice had seemed merely a walk round the aisles. She was unprepared for

'With my body I thee worship', remote from her feelings for Basil.

A shock too was the promise to obey. She mumbled the words. She'd had enough of obeying her father.

Finishing their indifferent meal, they left the dining room. A shabby rug on the highly polished floor slipped from under Basil's feet. He managed to grab a doorknob, though wrenching his painful foot. The landlady Mrs Willoughby swanned out of a side room with exaggerated concern. 'I'm so sorry, too much polish! I make a god of my home you see!' To Cath it seemed a threadbare shrine for so much devotion. She watched Basil stagger up the stairs like a geriatric, still clutching their case, though she'd tried to take it. She guessed rightly there'd be no sex that night.

The cries of gulls awakened Cath early. Pantiled roofs were bright outside.

'Look Basil!' she called, 'Pillars and pediments! Classical doorways on every house.'

'What's so wonderful?' was his put down, 'Come back to bed!'

He was on form again, though his touch was hardly sensitive. As he groaned to his climax, a silent Cath heard footsteps on the stairs.

Later, she waited in the digs for Basil, shopping for a film for his camera. She glanced at framed photos of a dark eyed man. One was on the mantle shelf, others on the glossy sideboard.

'Do you know the Willoughby's of York?' asked the landlady, picking up one of the portraits.

'I'm afraid not.'

'No? My husband's a distant relative of theirs.' Mrs Willoughby went on, lingering over the photo. Cath thought the relationship very distant, judging by the highly polished junk, though she sensed the woman's adoration of her man.

She noticed a sepia bride in a twenty's frame.

'My only daughter.' Mrs. Willoughby explained.

'She spent her honeymoon here too.' Looking closely at Cath, she added

'They spent the whole fortnight in their room, just surfacing for meals.'

Cath reddened, as Basil entered to collect her. Later, wandering past brightly painted boats, a heavy disappointment slowed her steps.

Cath watched the fishing boats alone next day. Women being barred from the Jolly Sailor's tap room, Basil had insisted that she wait outside.

'So much for not obeying.' she thought. She could have drunk in the Public Bar on her own, but the little cash she had saved was gone. Basil wasn't forthcoming with any more. When he finally came out, they walked up the steep path to the Abbey. Now breathless from the walk, Cath sank onto the green of its lawns. She watched white clouds pass tall arches, the gold of their frames arching towards blue. Flooded by sudden longing, Cath reached towards Basil beside her, but ignoring her, he stood up. Glancing briefly at the ruin, he started towards the town, calling

'Get up and let's get some grub! I've seen enough of this religious crap.' Clouds gathered and warmth drained from the scene.

After Edna's removal to Lulu's, Rita had thoughts of creating two flats at 11 Windsor Drive. Refurbishing in the new style would, she hoped, erase memories lingering in the cluttered rooms. Basil and Cath would rent the downstairs flat, keeping the sideboard minus its mirror, plus an old suite from the attic. Lulu had taken the old 'drawing room' contents, so this would serve as their bedroom. Basil papered the front room in Regency stripes, to tone with the turquoise tiles of the great fireplace. It assumed a surprising elegance in its new surround. The Edwardian attic suite, echoed the colour of the new velvet curtains, paid for by Bert. Cath loved it after living in digs.

However, it didn't turn her into a model of housewifery. As Basil's father had predicted, her asthma prevented frenetic activity with hoover and duster. Her mastery of the culinary arts was slow. She lost awareness of the passing of time, as the unstructured days merged together. When she'd managed to light the coal fire, she read books and daydreamed for hours. Her reverie penetrated by the striking of her father's old clock, she would realise the time. Basil would he home. She would struggle to get together a meal. Halfway through the process, Basil would rush through the door shouting

'Get that bloody tea on the table!' He had pain between meals but wouldn't see a doctor.

'What the hell do you do all day anyway,' he often raged, scraping at the unpolished floor for fluff.

'The place is a muck heap! I should have listened to my father!' In a guilty silence, Cath fumbled at the stove while he carried on.

On most evenings they sat together in the warmth, reading or listening to records. As the coals glowed in the pillared hearth, Cath felt a closeness to Basil. On other nights, the ones she dreaded, Basil's anger took off. Built up by frustration at the studio, at home it erupted like lava. Until three or four in the morning he ranted at the capitalist system, the Tory press, that pig and that bitch upstairs! Cath feared that Bert and Rita would hear, but it seemed the house was well built.

The couple showed up at Young Communist meetings, where they felt at home with the maladjusted crowd. A coach trip was put on to Rievaulx Abbey and the eighteenth century Rievaulx Terrace. Contributions of food were asked for, and Cath decided on a coffee cake from her economical cook book. It wasn't exactly money saving, being full of brown sugar and rich ingredients, but it looked gorgeous. The sense of achievement surprised Cath. Rain teemed at the start of the journey. Cath was afraid that Basil would plunge into a depression or tower into a rage, but thankfully he seemed unusually calm. Cora's boyfriend Morris, on his own, came late and had to sit next to Jocelyn Clifford. Her Oxford tones scintillated sharply among the flattened vowels around her. True to her Marxist convictions she had taken up an ill paid job in the most working class area she could find. She was a weaver in a Huddersfield woollen mill, though it was hard to imagine the management placing her in the role. On Saturday mornings she stood outside Woolworth's, to the crowd's amusement. Her cries of Daily Worker rang out clearly, though few copies sold.

As the coach moved northward the sky cleared. Cath, sleeping briefly, awoke to a seeming dream. The abbey remains, distant gold among green, stayed with them as they rounded a curve. They neared and, viewing its patterned walls, ate a communal lunch. Later through trees, they glimpsed the Rievaulx terrace. At either end of a sweep of lawn were its two temples, Tuscan and Ionic. Reaching there, they saw below a slope, the rising abbey arches. Lingering behind to be alone there, Cath envisioned, among columns, the lascivious glance of a Lovelace. As a leaf brushed her arm, she felt the delicate touch of Parson Yorick .... As she hurried to catch up with the group, poor Basil, stumbling in the rear, seemed a pathetic clown.

Quantities of the local mild and bitter were consumed on the way back. As they grew more communicative, Morris confided to Basil that Jocelyn had asked him to father her a child.

'Why pick on me?' he had asked her, 'Why not Basil or Harry Pollit? Or do you just think you won't be fertile much longer?'

He was shouting by now. Jocelyn, sitting a few seats behind, feared the whole coach had heard. If so they were past remembering.

That night Cath dreamed of stepping into a Watteau painting. In the warmth of late afternoon, groups of figures abandoned their still life. Pleasure stirred among satin clad limbs and the froth of lace. Cath felt hands and lips search with a timeless joy....... Wakening, she woke Basil. 'Get back to sleep!' he grunted, 'There's a time and place for everything.' As he dropped into sleep, her flame turned to ash.

Basil wanted children and couldn't imagine why Cath wasn't keen.

'The girls on our estate think of nothing but babies and weddings. I thought that was what we got wed for.' he went on.

'Half of them are pregnant at the alter.' Cath said, thinking of smirking brides with sheepish spouses. It was never long before the smiles were reversed. Cath had little desire for children. The more she saw of Basil, the less the desire grew. She didn't cherish the prospect of any like him, their small faces echoing his angry vindictiveness. Nor any with her own mask of tragedy.

Chapter 13

Tired of being roused by libidinous novels, with only Basil for company, Cath decided to look for a job. Putting together some sample book illustrations and visuals with scraps from her CPF waste paper basket, she set off. She got patronising refusals from several printers who never even looked at her work. Then the owner of a small studio actually consented to do so. A balding, heavy browed man, he reminded Cath strongly of her father. He arranged for her to start next Monday.

She pattered down rickety stairs into the street with rapid heartbeats, as she visualised drawing such objects as heavy goods vehicles without a reference. It had been gospel at college that references were out. She worried that they wouldn't be available. Figures and scenes from memory were reasonable, but she paled at the thought of machinery. An image of the man's brows bunching into a frown as he taunted her, kept her awake that night. In the morning she rang and ended the arrangement, much to her later regret.

Seeing a wanted ad for workers in a fireworks factory, Cath applied and was taken on. The factory was on bleak moorland some distance from Huddersfield, only a few cottages being in its vicinity. It only gradually dawned upon Cath that this isolation was due to possible explosions. The place had a prison like look. Cath worked with two other women, Marian about thirty and Joyce in her fifties. On piece rates, they worked incredibly fast, or so it seemed to Cath, paid by the hour.

There were so many odd characters at the factory that Cath felt relatively normal. One looked and smelled trampish.
'Keep away from her. She wets herself!' whispered Joyce.
'She can't help it, poor thing.' excused Marian. The place seemed a refuge for outcasts of all kinds. It wasn't long before Cath noticed, in the bus queue, a pair of women in men's belted macs. Their haircuts, 'short back and sides', suggested they were lesbians, creatures of fable to Cath.
'They have their rows. They're as jealous as any married couple. They

don't mind who knows about them here.' Marian told Cath.

'You want to watch it!' Joyce added, 'If they see anybody they fancy, they're after them.'

Mice thrived among the sacks of explosives, even rats it was rumoured. From a rustling waste bin Marian picked up an apparent mouse.

'That's no mouse – it's a young rat!' she declared, claiming that she could tell by its tail.

Cath wasn't bothered by this. They had mice at 11 Windsor Drive, but when she mentioned rats to Rita and Bert they blew up.

'You can't go on at that place!'

'Mice are one thing and rats another!' When Rita's brother offered Cath a job at his chemists', to their annoyance she refused. She had never handled cash and might face humiliating failure. At Flash Fireworks she was one of the peculiar crowd

Morris had persuaded Cora to begin treatment with a psychiatrist. A colleague of his own Doctor Isaacs, Henderson was known for his treatment of asthma. After several free association sessions, he felt that Cora was not a hysteric like his previous asthmatics, but an obsessional neurotic, more difficult to treat. Morris was aggrieved when the only result of the sessions so far was that Cora broke with him, on her psychiatrist's advice!

In spite of Cath's new contributions, the couple's income was still abysmal. As Christmas neared, she ordered a chicken well in advance. She was looking forward to the holiday feasting. As well as the iced cake and pudding, she had made some small mince pies and two larger apricot pies on saucers. On Christmas Eve she soon left the rowdy goings on at the factory to prepare the bird, only to find that Basil had swapped it for a rabbit and a bottle of red wine!

Furious at first, Cath was glad of the wine. On Christmas Day, they sat down to roast rabbit with all the trimmings, Brussels sprouts, sausage meat and two kinds of stuffing. Pudding and rum sauce followed. It was surprisingly good. Drowsy, they huddled round the fire, reading the books they had given each other.

During coffee breaks at Flash Fireworks, Marian and friends rehashed their nightly sexual delights.

'Five minutes, that's all it took last night. Five minutes!' laughed one.' All of an hour' said another 'Ecstasy every second!' Cath said nothing, the revelations confirming what her own marriage lacked. No wonder she'd felt depressed..... She confided the problem to the older Joyce.

'Just pretend to enjoy it. Love' she advised. Why pretend out of consideration for him, when he didn't consider her? Cath began to fantasise about finding another man. At least it might prove that she wasn't frigid, as Basil implied.

She arranged a night out with Marian. It was to be just a pub crawl, but Basil blazed up, though he'd taken to nights at their local himself.

'It's different for women.' he yelled. 'You might get picked up!'

Snapping 'What if I do!' Cath left.

In new clothes and heavy make up, she set off to meet Marian in the Queen's Hotel lounge. Excited, she strolled across the deep piled carpet to the highly polished bar for drinks. Looking around, the men in their local worsted suits seemed to be partnered already. After a couple of whiskies Marian wanted to move.

'Even the barmaids look down their noses! Let's try the Crown and Anchor.'

Cath's high drained away as they entered the pub. She and Basil had been there with Morris and Cora. Though she had glanced enviously into the lounge, now that she was there, it was hardly better than the tap room. The stained red of carpets and seats seemed brash. The men crowding the bar had heads smothered in Brylcream, or natural grease. It certainly wasn't attractive. Engrossed in their sporting talk, they scarcely noticed the women, to Cath's relief. Married Marian wasn't looking for a man. She just wanted drinks and a natter.

After a few reminiscences Cath had grown silent and suggested they change to the Pack Horse. As its name suggested it dated from the previous century. Cath almost expected spitoons and sawdust. All she saw were old men in flat caps, though none too clearly by now. A few drinks later, she refused Marian's offer to go on to a club, deciding to get the bus home. Hardly remembering boarding it, she stared, disappointed, from its window.

Basil meanwhile, had been having his own night out. He'd left home in one of his moods. Starting with a pint locally at the Bull in t' Thorn. The talk turning to sex, his admission to a pathetic once a fortnight routine had caused jeers he couldn't forget. He'd wandered around town looking for excitement. Beginning to limp now, he noticed through an archway a lit up sign 'Pomegranates' and thought he'd explore its possibilities.

Realising as he got closer that it was a pricy looking club, he turned back, but a hand touched his shoulder. Smiling invitingly, the stranger asked

'Why not come in as my guest?' Curious but dubious Basil followed him in. Warmth and light rushed out to greet them, as they opened the door to an elegance new to Basil. Peach shaded lamps lit the room, furnished in Regency style. On the grey green walls matched by a carpet soft to the touch of Basil's now swollen foot, were gilt framed prints. The smallness of the room gave an intimate air.

It was early yet and only another two members were around. His new friend, named Eric it appeared, ordered a pink gin and Basil had the same. His usual pint of bitter would be inappropriate he felt. Eric spoke of his antiques business, adding

'I furnished the rooms here myself you know.' His forehead lined above his Paisley cravat, he lit up an expensive cigar. Basil was fascinated by his talk of buying and selling. He refused Basil's offer to buy drinks and seemed to be willing to pay all evening.

'Well, he can obviously afford it!' thought Basil, deciding to let him carry on. Several gins later the room had filled with new faces, all male, their outlines now rather blurred.

'Going well is it Eric?' asked one. Another winked.

'I tell you what!' Eric suddenly announced, 'Why don't we go to my place? You're fond of antiques and I could show you some wonderful stuff.' Basil took little persuading, remembering Cath's night on the town. As they rose to leave, he suppressed his anger at the thought of her, determined not to ruin his own evening. The night air was refreshing but cold. As the car heated up Basil revelled in the comfortable warmth, watching lighted windows flicker through a veiling of winter trees. Eric's shop had a prominent position in the village street. In its wide windows highly polished furniture shone in a street lamp's glow. Entering by a side door, Basil followed Eric up thickly carpeted stairs. In yet another regency room, Basil was flung among the cushions of an elegant sofa. Male kisses crushed his protesting lips.

Immediately in the grip of one of his rages, Basil ripped the thin arms away. Flinging Eric against a Grandfather Clock, he rushed down the stairs. In the street, the Westminster chimes still rang in his ears. A bus was just passing and, forgetting his limp, he jumped on.

Some weeks later, when the Spring sun paled through the smoke, Basil booked on a coach trip to York. They visited the Minster with its great rose window and walked along the medieval walls. Cath gazed eagerly over its parapet at the tree-shaded clerical roofs below. Their mellow tiles and gold green lawns had an ancient peace. She wanted to bathe in their glow, forget sooty Huddersfield... Her high faded when Basil insisted they economise by lunching at a tatty tea shop, instead of the classical hotel recommended by the coach driver. Its worn furniture and faded chintz, unchanged since the thirties, depressed Cath. Then she smelled the over cooked greens. She knew it was useless to protest, it was all they could afford.

In the afternoon, visiting a gallery, Basil enthused on Victorian seascapes.
'Realistic rubbish! What do you see in them?' Cath laughed scathingly. Expounding on the simplicity of late Turners in the next room, she ended with a lecture on the moderns, dredged up from the works of Bell and Fry. Basil said little until they were leaving.
'Thanks for the info, wherever you read it. I don't need a book to tell me what I like.'

'Just to tell you what to think!' Cath snapped.

Tired on the return journey, Basil had a dream. Walking at night along a New York street, he and Cath stopped at a bright shop window. Piled high with strange and brilliant fruits, it glowed with a sense of luxury and splendour. As he exclaimed in delight, he caught sight of Cath's face, eyebrows raised in a condescending sneer. She poured scorn on each of the bright fruits in turn. Before his gaze they shrivelled, as the lighted window darkened.

As the months dragged on, Cath confessed doubts about her marriage to Cora, who spoke of it to her psychiatrist. Curious, Dr. Henderson offered cut price consultations. As she left the third session, Cath decided to make it her last. Hurrying along the mosaic hallway and out into the Autumn morning, she mulled over the previous visits. The psychiatrist had continually advised against divorce. Insisting that she could never have strong sexual feelings, he talked of living in a dream world. She must realise that her dreams could never become reality. Cath couldn't accept this verdict. She had to have the freedom to prove it wrong. Preoccupied, her eye was caught by a sea of crab apples lying at her feet, crimson and gold among leaves. A sudden image of the rosy face of Marian at Flash Fireworks swept into consciousness, strangely emotive.

'Surely not love ......' Cath thought, her own cheeks reddening.

She quitted the factory the following Monday.

Basil was furious at Cath giving up her job. They needed the money and she had no explanation. They had planned to see 'Love on the Dole' at the Kozy Nook and went ahead despite the lack of funds. After queuing, an usherette led them to a back row double seat. It proved an embarrassing experience. The heavy breaths and groping hands all around reminded the pair how routine their lovemaking had become. Seated rigidly side by side, Cath's anger at her own situation soon became focused on the screen. She had not been keen to see the film, having read that the heroine had been given a posh accent and a ridiculous new name, Millie Southern. Apparently southerners couldn't identify with the northern heroine of the book! She hated the film, as she loathed Gracie Fields and George Formby.

Coming out into the frosty night air, they hurried to the Spotted Cow for a drink. The cold beer in the scarcely warm Tap Room did little to raise their spirits.

'All I want is lovin' you and music music music....' blared out the new juke box. Each sat silently. Cath finally voiced what had been on her mind for months.

'I want a divorce Basil.' she murmured, her voice so low that she feared having to repeat it. Basil had heard.

'You're not the only one!' he surprised her.

'I've been thinking the same. I'll have to look for some woman. We can't wait three years for a desertion decree.'

Waiting at a bus stop in the November chill, Cath glanced as a car pulled up. Inside, a man was delicately stroking a woman's cheek. Her face was lost in a passion Cath could only envy. She was sure she knew the man, but from where?

Cath and Cora wandered into Field's cafe where they still occasionally met. About to retreat as all tables were full, a voice called

'Come on twins and join us!'

It was Angela from art school, surrounded by friends, who made space on a settee for the pair.

'I'm just arranging my housewarming. Would you like to come?' Though Cora declined, Cath welcomed the invite – anything for a change from Basil. Angela and her architect husband were hosting the party at their new home. This was in a wing of a neo classical house, whose facade the twins had often seen beyond high walls, on their journeys to and from school. Basil at first refused to go, but thought he might meet some suitable female for a quick divorce.

Cath felt ridiculous in floral nylon, a survival from her honeymoon. Most women were wearing the new pencil slim dresses. Others had enormous skirts. Angela aimed at sophistication in slim line black, sleeveless, its huge white collar cut low. Joy and Vic were among the crowd, with other ex students less well remembered. A buffet table looked very tempting, piled with an excess of unfamiliar foods Cath sat stiffly on a delicate chaise longue, sipping at a glass of white wine. Basil clad in his father's demob suit, had had a few beers and lost his normal introversion. Positively manic, forgetting his foot, he partnered woman after woman. He was unaware of raised eyebrows, as guests wondered where this clownish redhead had sprung from.

Glancing through quickstepping forms, Cath became aware of a steady gaze. The stranger she had seen from the bus stop was making his way through the crowd with champagne. Fair hair fell over one blue eye as he joined her. Taking a glass Cath asked

'I know you from somewhere but where?'

'Art school and very much earlier.' he smiled. 'I was five when we met, but I still remember shy twins putting on new slippers....'

'Charles Swinburne Platt! Your mother's dance school.....' Cath recalled the snowy drive and the warm scented conservatory. As he spoke, his touch burned through the fabric of her sleeve. After partnering her through several dances, he propelled her silently up a flight of stairs. Then into a room. Through its window were a myriad coloured lamps in garden trees......

Finally they returned to the dancers, now jiving perilously near to expensive antiques. Cath was relieved that Basil, still busily gyrating, seemed not to have noticed her absence. As the dance ended, his partner rejoined her friends. Whispering, they glanced with amusement at Basil. They'd be married forever Cath thought, if she waited for him to find a corespondent.

Cath arranged coral cups on her coffee table, her hands alive with the sensuality new to her in the past few months. She had bought the tiny cups second hand, their rich tones bright as her joy, brief though she felt it might be. Charles's secret visits to Eleven Windsor Drive had made real what was earlier only glimpsed, in others' touches, glances. Now she feared he was tiring of her.

She sat and waited. The coffee grew cold in the pot. Charles had never stood her up before. Gripped by fear, she flung on a coat and left. Hardly aware, she drifted through Leighton Fields, seeking his mother's great house. Here Gloria Swinburne had reigned over her dance drama school. Clouds were gathering as Cath came within sight, though a shaft of sun swept over the lawns. Hesitant now, her steps slowed as a car shot past. Turning into the drive was Charles's familiar sports car. Smiling beside him was a blond, expensively dressed. Cath retreated, slowing to a seeming crawl.

Sure she wouldn't see him again, she had to know more. Angela would tell, but how humiliating. What about Joy? Feverishly she scanned the phone book. Joy came over and fresh coffee filled the coral cups.

'You're so naive Cath! What about Basil?' she asked.

'We want a divorce.' Cath confessed, 'I just wanted to know what I've been missing.'

'You could get more than you bargained for! He's known all over Huddersfield. Mostly for getting engaged to young girls and breaking it off. I've heard a breach of promise case is pending.'

'Do they still exist?' Cath murmured, an idea forming. He could be involved in a divorce case too. Basil was getting nowhere after all. Though Cath's new world had darkened, a cold resolve was growing. She forced herself to ring Charles and cajole him into another visit.

Drinking their coffee from the coral cups, the hand on Cath's thigh was no less arousing in spite of her change of feeling for Charles. Later, lost between covers, she was as shocked as her lover when doors were flung open and the prearranged detective burst in. Red cheeked, blond hair awry, Charles struggled into clothes as did Cath, before the interrogation began.

Chapter 14

A taxi arrived early at 11 Windsor Drive, for a silent Basil and his two small suitcases. Unemotional on his leaving, Cath broke into tears on seeing forgotten sandals, awaiting an owner who wouldn't return. She forced herself out of the house, to carry on with the job she had started that week, as a paid collector for an animal charity. The collectors were paid a percentage of their takings. Though she had worked nine to five each day except Sunday, the percentage had been pitifully small.

With a half full tin from an earlier collection, Cath boarded a bus for the Brackenridge Estate. Forcing back tears, she hurried past her father-in-law's home. Penetrating further into the enormous estate, welcoming smiles became rarer. One door was opened by a synthetic blond. Backed by upturned faces, she yelled

'We can't afford bloody bread, never mind charities! We could do with some charity 'ere.,'

'You can afford to dye your hair – that's more than I can' Cath called as she moved on. Many houses were empty, their tenants at work, but several streets further on, a face peered through the grime of a window. As Cath walked up the gateless path, the door was opened by a bare footed woman. Pushing back long matted hair, her gaze was unfocused. Inside, Cath saw on a bare concrete floor, a listless toddler beside a pile of its faeces. The woman remained mute as she closed her door. Though she looked crazy, Cath felt she was better alone than in the care of 'professionals'. She hurried away, deciding to quit the estate. Unsure of the way out, she stared around at broken fences and knee high grass thickly rimed with frost. Catching sight of a dog, she started towards it, thinking the owner might give to the charity. With a snarl, it hurtled towards her, only stopped by the length of its chain. Heart pounding, Cath turned and ran the length of the avenue, reaching the estate's outer limits. Beyond frosted slate roofs, mirror imaged semi-detached homes seemed safe in a disolving world.

Later Cath and Basil met at his father's, to discuss their divorce. They clung together crying, as the father commented

'You're like a couple of newly weds after a row! Are you sure you want a divorce?'

But they both knew there was no turning back.

Hardly able to eat on her share of the charity collection, Cath got together some new designs and planned a trek round the Manchester studios. To her surprise, she got work as a colourist at one of the largest, employing about twenty five staff. She started the job with some anxiety, as De Jardin's was known for demanding fast work.

Cath took a bedsitter in Victoria Park. Once elegant, its terraces now looked delapidated. After an exhausting climb to the two attic rooms, Cath would spend most evenings in the tiny warm kitchen. Wrapped around by the heat of an oil stove, through books she would enter other realities. She discovered a nearby delicatessen. She delighted in trying their interesting foods, strange breads, cheesecakes, rollmops.

Cath found the girls at Francois De Jardin's very different from her fellow workers at the C.P.F. To the Top Twenty hits, they joked and chattered continuously, except at a tap on the door from De Jardin's secretary.

A whispered 'D's up!' was passed from table to table and the room became quiet as a morgue.

'I'm off to the remnant shop to buy some material. I saw it last week, in the new sage green.' announced Vivien the head colourist excitedly.

'Mum gave me lunch money,' she went on 'but I got up early and made some jam sarnies. It's five-to-twelve girls, let's eat.'

Opening her lunch box as 'D's up!' buzzed around the room, in a flash it was hidden away.

No luck for Jan. Spots of mayonnaise dropped on her work.

'What is zis?' cried De Jardin,

'Zat's a week's work wasted!'

Frantic as mayonnaise smeared his tailor made suit, he screamed

'You're ruining my business!' Jan froze like a cornered mouse, but Vivien's quick work with a sponge got rid of the offending spots. 'D' calmed down and in the hushed room, carried on with his critical round.

By degrees, Cath let slip details of her marriage and divorce to the girls. Jan confessed to doubts about her fiancee,

'I don't like to get too close......' she explained.

'I can't get close enough!' commented Vivien.

Cath urged Jan to finish with him while there was still time. To the girls' surprise, the next week, Jan announced that the engagement was off. She suggested that she and Cath should go dancing that Saturday, at the Willoughby Lodge Hotel. Turning the corner into Willoughby Road with Jan, Cath caught her first glimpse of the hotel. Jewel lamps hung on the trees bordering the winding drive. Twin globes lit a flight of steps. Light flooded from the entrance hall. The rich scent of brandy and spirits recalled Cath's first Masonic party. It shone star bright down the wasted years.

Later, elation flagged as the women hung around until asked to dance. Most male faces looked coarse, others old in close up. Thirty seemed the average age, though many were forty or more.

'Married men on the loose.' whispered Cath, as disappointment set in.

The two women had a few dances, but not with anyone remotely of interest. As the 'last waltz' ended, they hurried out to catch a late bus.

'At least my age was no problem there.' Cath remarked, conscious of her twenty five years.

Cath spent odd weekends at Lulu's in Huddersfield. Their mother's miraculous cure carried on, but Cath felt grief at the change in Cora. Skeletally thin, her cheeks and lips had a bluish tinge and she weighed less than six stone. The twins weren't identical anymore. Cora had given up her psychiatrist, her asthma wasn't responding. When the analysis had thrown up her hatred of their father, she had hated the disloyalty. Emphysema was preferable to guilt. Now a Catholic, she had thoughts of a convent, but a medical was standard even there. She had made a gooseberry tart for Cath's visit. She and Cath ate a large slice each, but no one else did.

'Why don't any of you eat what I make?' she asked.

'We'll have some bye and bye.' Edna answered, but it was left in the fridge until mouldy.

Coughing and spitting into a cup as prescribed, Cora felt their disgust. Cath was glad she had cast off the family. It drained Cora's life like a strangulating vine.

From Huddersfield, Lulu rang cousins in Manchester and arranged a visit for Cath. She found herself on a street whose further end seemed at vanishing point. Built of brick, the slate roofs were echoed in miniature roofs over windows and doors. Here and there, bombed out buildings were replaced by a semi detached pair, breaking the harsh parallels. From a slate sky rain began, as Cath finally found the house.

The door was opened by Cousin Brenda, her face framed by thirties style waves. They passed through an entrance hall into a kitchen, warm from a fire in a black leaded range. A Labrador lay on a peg rug, at the feet of Alec Munroe. His hair, in the same miniature waves as his wife's, gave them a curious similarity.

'Welcome to our home Cath. 'Brenda's husband Jim greeted her with a smile, as he shook hands and kissed her on the cheek.

With his high tenor charm he seemed about to break into song.....

'How are Auntie Edna and the rest of the family?' asked Brenda.

'I scarcely hear anything of the aunties.' Cath answered, giving what little she knew of the Hunts these days.

As conversation flagged, the couple left the room, whispering in the hallway.

'It's your turn to get supper.'

'She's your relative!'

Later a smiling Brenda returned, followed by Alec with tea and rather stale cakes. Cath didn't linger too long, not feeling genuinely welcome.

Cath wasn't finding the work at De Jardin's too easy. The asthmatic heaving of her chest caused slower than normal speed. Though asked, she didn't join the others in their lunch hour jaunts, unable to walk at their speed, due to her asthma. She also felt an oddity, in that most of the girls were on an apprenticeship scheme, different for men and women. The boys began immediately on setting to repeat, starting on designing in just two years. The girls spent two years on colourings and three years on setting to repeat, before they were given a chance to design. The young girls seemed content with the system,

'Don't you think it's unfair?' Cath asked, but they turned on her.

'We won't need to work when we're married.' said one.

'Men are the breadwinners!' trotted out another. The two older designers, one single and one married, expressed no opinion.

Designing needed intense concentration. All the new designs done at the studio were based loosely on styles from the French ateliers. The two designers did their excellent work, in spite of the chatter and the blare of the radio. Its output varied from the schmaltz to the brash.

Max Miller's 'My mother's pearls are her boys and her girls.' brought hoots of derision.

'She wore red feathers and a hula, hula skirt.' was popular.

The connecting door to the men's studio was always firmly closed. Even so, Mike the head designer often entered explosively.

'Cut the damned racket! Some of us are doing serious work.'

Cath's friend Jan in her fifth year, was promoted to designing. Her nights out with Cath at the Willoughby Lodge soon finished, as she was seen around with a designer from the studio. Cath carried on alone with the Willoughby evenings.

That Saturday, a tall figure emerged from the crowd and asked her for a dance. Coming closer, he looked well over six foot, but they danced together surprisingly well. When asked to his flat for coffee, Cath was about to refuse, but wine and attraction won her over. As they entered a driveway, light shone from pointed windows. In a first floor room, a marble fireplace threw out welcoming warmth. Mark brought Drambuie from a cupboard, its arches high as those framing the outer blue. Cath took a glass, its fieriness shocked, but gradually its subtle flavour appealed to her. As the bottle slowly emptied an arm crept about her, a hand was in her dress. Lost in the glow of the fire, the whisky, she was swept from her feet towards a bedroom, the whiteness of sheets. Though longing to stay, she knew she must leave.

Insisting 'Let me down.', she slipped from his grasp.

He stared as she headed for the stairs.

'I thought it was what you wanted.' he murmured, as he followed her down.

Driving her home, they arranged another meeting.

Cath meant to insist on going out on the Saturday, resisting the temptation of Mark's flat. But when he phoned the studio on the Wednesday, she agreed to meet him that evening.

'We don't want your men phoning here!' frowned the head designer.

He had hinted already that her speed was below par. Also, De Jardin being Catholic, most of the girls were from convent schools. Could she be seen as a threat to their virtue? Cath wondered.

Her confidence was low that evening, as she hurried to the waiting car. It looked in need of a clean. She fancied Mark's glance at her unwashed hair and she didn't have the nerve to insist on going out. Soon they were approaching the towered and pinnacled dwelling, silhouetted against a lowering sky. She wasn't up to resisting Mark, though his rooms were cold and excitement minimal. They left the flat with scarcely a word. Passing the Drambuie cupboard, carved corbels drooped disconsolately. A house mite scurried through the surface dust. Deposited on the corner of her terrace, Cath knew she'd seen the last of the car and its driver.

Through the following weeks, she haunted The Willoughby Lodge on Saturdays, but Mark never reappeared. Against Summer skies, the coloured lamps left a trail of pain, on each lone return to her rooms. While working on her colourings at De Jardin's, memories of her first evening with Mark defied concentration. Such images glowed among dark fears of a solitary future. Weeks passed and fear of pregnancy began to swamp all other emotions. Fortunately the fear proved unfounded. Gradually the memory of Mark faded.

Cath went less often to the Willoughby Lodge. She was sickened by greasy hair, greasy suits, inane remarks such as

'You're a dark horse you are!', at the mention of books, theatres, concerts.

Mature, interesting looking men ignored her. In any case, they probably had wives. Marriageable men seemed impossible to find, while a permanency of life in two rooms on a colourist's wage, was hardly an enviable prospect.

Cath thought of other areas of human contact, local politics, perhaps. Suspecting that her role would be making cups of tea while men spouted, the idea lost its appeal. Finally joining a dramatic society, she began work on a back cloth for 'The Cherry Orchard' without much enthusiasm, (she seemed unable to enthuse about anything). Jan recommended a music club which Cath joined. Though she tried to lose herself in the recordings, she couldn't ignore the distance she felt between herself and this cosily respectable crowd.

Eventually, a decree absolute finalised Cath's divorce and she returned to her premarital name. Being Miss Hunt could cut out the need for embarrassing explanations. So at any rate she hoped.

On one of Cath's visits to her cousin, Brenda confided that Alec had TB and was in a Lake District sanatorium. Here they were trying out the new antibiotics. She suggested Cath should live at their home, at least during his treatment. With nothing to lose Cath moved in. Brenda's cool, unsentimental outlook reminded Cath of her sister-in-law Rita, though she was far from having Rita's culinary skills. Tea was at four for their five year old, Bruce, its remains being reheated for Cath. She didn't relish these rehashed meals, but they were well worth putting up with for the company.

One weekend, Cath helped Bruce to make a great jewelled crown from coloured paper and foil.

'I'm the King, I'm the King, I'm the King of the Castle!' he shouted, startling the old Labrador as he jumped on her back.

His flushed cheeks and fever bright eyes, were in contrast to his withdrawn gaze on return from his private school. At home too, Brenda kept to Alec's severe regime in his absence. At mealtimes Bruce would call

'Excuse me! Excuse me!' before being allowed to speak.

He seemed friendless. Primary school children jeered at the school-capped little figure at Brenda's side. Cath found herself becoming fond of little Bruce.

At De Jardin's, Jan now engaged, lent Cath an old union card, to try out the University dances. Cath had just received her yearly sum of thirty pounds – her share of the rent from some family property. With this, she had bought three dress lengths and a coat, handbag and shoes. Several weeks work had seen this material made up into dresses, which she was quite looking forward to wearing, especially at a new venue. As the work progressed, Brenda brought out a suit, about twenty years old by its style.

'Alec's always been fond of this suit, I wore it on our honeymoon.'

'It's lovely material.' said Cath, dreading what would come next.

'Do you think you could alter it, make it more modern?' Brenda asked.

'I could try.' Cath felt forced to answer, though she knew she couldn't modernise the bias cut panels.

She hoped Brenda would forget the project.

As Cath set off for the University dance, she felt good in her polished cotton dress, jacket over arm. The dress featured a black and white design with a mushroom ground, though the neck had turned out lower than intended. It revealed a less than modest cleavage. The sense of guilt she felt at using another's card soon passed, as she talked to a group of women students. They seemed quite friendly, but when she looked back at them while dancing, their derisive glances were unmistakable.

'Very provocative!' one remarked, glancing down at Cath's low cut dress, where a fraying bra strap poked out.

Though she hid it, their laughter still rang in her ears, in spite of the vocalist and twenty piece band. She danced several times, but finding that she wasn't on a college course, her partners drifted away. The sea of faces looked incredibly young. An antique at twenty six, Cath left for home.

Missing a bus, she bought a coffee at the bus station bar. While she drank, four men jumped out of a battered white van and got drinks.

'You're late tonight Love.' one said, 'You've an hour to wait. There's nothing now 'til the all night buses start.'

'Leave her alone Harry, haven't you had enough for one night? 'asked another.

A suspicious looking bunch she decided, but one had a strong appeal. Dark eyes, nose scimitar curved. He turned, gave a long glance then looked away. They began talking about bus times. With an hour to wait, though doubtful, Cath took up their offer of a lift. Two of the group seemed hardly memorable, but no eye could ignore Harry. A crew cut, unnaturally blond, topped his heavy lidded face, white in the fluorescent glare. He wore a teddy boy suit of a delicate blue. Cath felt relief at seeing Danny, the quiet attractive one, climb into the driving seat. It appeared they lived in Clapham Hill, on a bus route passing along Willoughby Road. Dropping her off at her cousin's, Danny asked

'There's a party on Thursday, shall we pick you up at eight?'

Nodding her assent, Cath hurried in.

Danny's remembered image did nothing to help Cath complete her six colourings a day. Hearing about last night's meeting, Jan warned

'That bus station bar's got a terrible reputation!'.

Another girl went on 'I wouldn't go out with anybody I met there!'

All the same that evening, Cath waited impatiently for the sound of the van. She was wearing another of her new dresses, rather more sophisticated she hoped, in slate grey with a pencil slim skirt. As the white van drew up she ran out, her cousin, curious, following behind. Catching sight of the faces peering through a window, Brenda whispered

'Don't go!'.

But, almost losing her high heeled shoes, Cath had already clambered up beside Danny. They set off at speed.

Now wishing she had taken the advice, Cath saw Danny openly go through crossing after crossing at red.

Yells of 'Come on man!'

'Get the next one the next one!' drowned the engine's roar.

They soon pulled up at a depressing brick pub, reeking of stale beer as they entered. The big bar with its yellowing walls seemed cold and cheerless to Cath. Many seats were empty and she saw no other women. She wondered vaguely about the promised party as she put on her jacket.

It could get colder when she poured her drink down. Almost tripping over the worn carpet, she followed in the wake of the men.

The group around a long corner table greeted them, as Harry, the zoot suited blond, ordered drinks all round.

'What d' you think Fellers? I'm on the booze again!' he smiled, raising his pint high, to cheers.

'Good lad!' called a friend 'Back with the girls again eh?'

'Starting tonight man!' laughed Harry, winking at Cath. From a buzz of voices, she picked out words such as discharge, contact and a few women's names. Bonnie's friend Sylvia flashed through her mind, as with instant awareness, she saw syphilitic features among the men. Recalling with mounting anxiety the old V.D. posters, she cursed her stupidity. Murmuring of a need for the Ladies, she quietly made her way to a side door.

Hope revived in the fresh wind. The still blue sky was darkening, as lamps were lit. Before Cath could mount a slowing down bus, arms dragged her into the reappearing van. Danny wasn't there, just Harry and two of the venereal crowd.

'To your uncle's, OK?' asked the driver.

'That's right, he's away all week,' Harry answered 'but move!'

With a screech of brakes Cath was bundled from the vehicle and through the front door of a dilapidated house. She was flung on a sofa in a room smelling of drink. In a dream like suspension of space and time, she was aware of pulling and mauling. Twisting her legs around each other, fear of the pox held them rigid as steel. The ceiling rose swam in its whiteness. Hands dragged and tore at her clothes, tore at their own, in brutal attempts at rape. Harry was almost there, to cries of

'Be quick man!'

'Me next!', when the outside door burst open...... With

'What d' you think this is, a knocking shop?' Harry's uncle stormed in.

As he went on 'Bringing your tarts in!' Cath dragged herself through the hallway and out of the still open door.

Almost slipping, she scrambled onto a bus, terrified the van would reappear.

Her unseeing eyes stared through the bus's misted windows. Tall terraces of flats and rooming houses swam past, as a shifting crowds got on and off. Supressing tears, she clasped her shaking hands. As they passed the long gardens of Willoughby road, she wondered at the lives of those behind the glowing windows. They might have belonged to some other planet for all the kinship she felt. On the unbroken route, she had soon reached the Munroe's neighbourhood. She fastened her jacket and turned up its collar, hoping to conceal her torn dress.

Letting herself in at her cousins, she poked her head around the kitchen door. All was in darkness, Brenda being long since in bed. The old Labrador bitch jumped guiltily off one of the chairs, but settled herself comfortably back, as Cath silently crept up the stairs.

Though she tried to take the night's happehings in her stride, she was conscious of a gathering desperation. She never completed the 'Cherry Orchard' backcloth, though guilty at letting the theatre club down. On her return, others had finished the work.

When Brenda next visited the sanatorium, Cath dropped in on a Congregational service. Hatless and wind tossed, her brown locks raised eyebrows. The women vied with each other in an elaboration of head wear. Did it occur to them, Cath wondered, that the female covering of heads was to mark their inferiority to men, in the sight of their Lord? Feeling again unwelcome, she didn't return to the fold.

Increasingly isolated, Cath bought Pelican books on psychology, but recalling her mother's experience, avoided asking for help. She couldn't bear the thought of years in a mental institution. There would be no means of exit, no goal or stimuli to break the endless circling of thought. Eventually, she joined a social club. Known as 'Willoughby Rd. Eighteen Plus Group', most of its members were pushing thirty. Here at least she felt less of a freak, others were survivors of broken relationships. One man led a desperate existence, dossing in a rented shack that doubled as a radio repair shop. Another, working as a fitter but constantly sacked, confessed to a dread of ending up homeless.

Alec was now home from the sanatorium. Finishing the last of her home sewn dresses, Cath was shocked at his sudden outburst.

'You never did alter that suit of Brenda's!' he shouted, throwing aside his Daily Mail. 'You're utterly and entirely selfish and you think about nothing but men!'

'It just can't be done.' Cath told him. It's cut on the bias and can't be made straight. I'm sorry.'

'You could have told her.' he snapped, flouncing from the room.

Cath was shocked again at a neighbour's verdict.

Remarking to Brenda 'Cath looks very smart these days.'

She added 'Where does the money come from? Is she on the game?'

On Sundays, the group members went rambling. With them, fortified by ephedrine for her asthma, Cath traversed the Pennine foothills. She enjoyed these Sundays whether it rained or shone. They boosted her flagging self esteem. She even began to feel her cousin's place was home and asked if she could put on a party for the group. Brenda's cold reply was

'You're only a lodger!'

Chapter 15

At eight thirty Cath caught the Newcastle bus. Settling into her seat, she saw A.G. Kent (as she always thought of him) on his daily walk to his office. It was some years since she had last done work for him. He seemed changed and not for the better.

'That bloke's going bonkers.' Alan had said, as he saw him passing their house. He certainly did look odd. He stared wide eyed as he walked, with a nervous jerk now and then, as if a sound had interrupted his thoughts. She caught a glimpse of his teeth. Though few now, no dentures had filled the gaps. His hair was short now and grey, his sinewy neck vulture like, as his coat collar flapped in the wind. Everyone changes she thought, look at herself. Before long she might not see him with any sort of clarity. Though since the laser treatment two years ago her eye hadn't worsened. She still hoped for no change.

Gazing out of the bus window at the Tyne, across fields bordered by tree covered slopes, Cath recalled a walk she had taken that Summer. She had come upon what she thought of as 'the house with the Chinese garden'. Walking up a steep rise on the outskirts of the town, its red tiled roof had swum into view past the slate and stone of a terrace. It was a large bungalow, thirties detached, aloof on the brow of the hill. At each point of its roof, a curious incurving ridge tile held something strangely Oriental. As she climbed higher, incredibly, two great stone blocks had appeared. Each on a plinth, their surfaces writhed with a Chinese intensity of dragons and fish. They had seemed more strange against pristine lawns and newly turned borders. Behind the house had spread only the sky, to the right a footpath and fields. Inquisitive, she had followed the path. At the back a French window viewed a neat garden. Below, minute, were the roofs of the town and the tree shaded Abbey. Behind the low wall the hillside dropped sharply. The path becoming steep, Cath had retraced her steps to a more gradual road. Curious, she had entered an interesting archway, to find a great quarry, disused now with blackening stone. Wild vegetation grew in its crevices. Raising her eyes she had seen, above its height, the roof tiles of the 'house with the Chinese garden.'

Alighting from the bus on its arrival in Newcastle, Cath passed rough looking pubs and cafes. Most signs, on white plastic, were supplied by a Cola company complete with its logo. A newsagents' window was crowded with posters and cards with items for sale. The upper rooms of tall buildings were empty, their windows dirty and dark. Torn newspapers flapped desultorily along the worn pavement. She turned a corner to the pleasanter view of trees and a newly cleaned church. On the left a hotel had been gutted and formed the facade of a new block of flats. It had been an odd combination of classical symmetry and art nouveau glass. As a mature student, she had rushed to take photos when alterations began.

Cath made her way to the Hanover Press. Planning a new print, she got out some old photos and started to work out ideas. A visiting American was working on one of his latest abstractions. Using ink on a zinc plate, he had painted a line 3 inches from each edge. Mixing a few colours he filled up the outer area with brush strokes, stolidly and deliberately placed. With a larger brush and the same deliberation, he filled up the centre. Placing the plate, with paper and blanket, on a large etching press, he printed and pulled out his large monoprint. After gazing at it to his own satisfaction, he started to wander around. Casting his eye over one of Cath's prints he remarked, in his drawn out nasal tones,
'There's gallery art and there's dining room art!'

On a prepared plate Cath worked on a new print. In it, in her father's open car, the couple were arriving at a mental institution. Heavy clouds and crazily twisted trees towered over the monstrous place. Cath hoped to convey her mother's emotions, though not expecting great sales. Surprisingly, she had sold quite a few of the prints of her mother's breakdown. The drama of the too small pie went down well with social workers. Cath wanted to get these prints of her mother out of the way before starting on the lives of herself and her twin. Whether they sold or not, she saw them as important to the twins' own story.

As she carried on working Roy Clement came in. He had changed, was anxious, pale and on crutches. He started a whispered conversation with a friend. Cath heard fragments but couldn't get the gist of what had happened.

'When I jumped...', 'multiple injuries...'

It seemed he had injured himself by a fall from a bridge. She felt sorry. He had been the first one there to encourage her. She would have loved to find out details, but she was never one to pry. He left the area and she heard nothing more.

Cath decided to try another place, a new night spot open for lunch. Coming in from strong sunlight, the place had a subterranean gloom. To the right on raised platforms were dark polished tables and bentwood chairs. Large potted plants, luxurious though fake, gave an intimate feel under fan shaped lamps. High tinted windows splashed purples and pinks. On the left were the buffet and bar, its dark curves hinting at Jugendstil. Colourful salads reappeared in sparkling mirrors. Cath seated herself with a salad filled bun. She couldn't resist adding coffee and cream. Looking around, she peopled the room with its night time crowd, including her son who came here.

Coming out into the street the wind was stronger. Hair blowing over her good eye left the faulty one showing her a dreamlike haze. She headed for the new shopping centre. Clad in subtly toned brick, its interesting shapes would appear unexpectedly in widely spaced parts of the city. Through a glass door and up an escalator she arrived at the main shopping mall. She liked to see the young of the moment, their changing hairstyles and clothes. In passing she glanced at the shops' signs and windows, designed to entice the youngsters.

Entering Boots, Cath made her way to their framed print department. She had recently sent marker visuals to a London commercial print company. They had written of giving her a commission, but would like to see finished work. To this end Cath was looking around various stores, comparing the latest framed prints. The visuals she had sent were in airbrush style, finished versions of some being ready. A few more would be enough to send off. She hardly dared hope for success, though she'd worked hard at getting the right look.

Before this, Cath had worked free-lance for a local mining group. She redesigned leaflets and added new ones to the range. Deadlines had to be met. With her part-time job at a Party Plan company, she had time for little else but work. It filled weekdays, evenings and weekends for weeks at a time. She hardly saw Alan and the kids. Finally it was too much. She just kept the party plan work. Other opportunities followed. She enjoyed display work for a local store, but when she refused a job because of a family holiday, there was no more work from that source! It was then that she had begun her own prints at the Hanover. She even tried her hand at sign-writing on a door, amused by the disbelieving stares of passers by. Looking back on it all though, she'd never earned real money. Perhaps that would change, if she got a commission from the London print group.

There had been experiences that still rankled. Especially one in the foyer of an advertising agency. While they waited for interviews, a man about thirty without any work, had chatted about his ten years in a garage after leaving art college. Her interview was for two thirty, his at three, but he was whisked off at two on a tour of the studios. He was given the job without having shown any work. Cath picked up her folder and asked

'Why haven't I been seen. She was stunned at the reply from the boss.

'I thought you were somebody's mother sat there. We've interviewed several young people today.'

Unable to think of a biting reply, she picked up her folder and left.

Wandering past the shopping mall windows, Cath thought she would look for some holiday clothes. It was depressing. There was little in size eighteen. The dress in khaki with red sleeves and trim had looked great. It looked so balloonish when she got it on that she felt about to take flight. She couldn't be bothered to return it. At college she had dieted and lost three stones, thinking it might get her a job. There seemed little point in trying it now. She had wondered if the diet could have caused her vision loss. Her GP had avoided an answer.

Cath decided she had time to visit her favourite book shop. Dating from the mid nineteenth century, the shop had several departments. She wasn't intending to buy, just to look.

'Don't go buying a load of books.' said Allan 'The library's the place for them.'

To him money was there to save.

'For what?' Cath would say, but got no answer.

To her it was there to spend on pleasure, when you'd covered the bare necessities. There was something special about a new book, a paperback with its glossy cover and sharply cut edges, smelling so delightfully new. She glanced through a book on the delicate Rajput paintings of India and one on the architecture of Islam. This had been a revelation when she first saw it on early television.

She recalled the books she had bought with her college grant, illustration books with strange names and strange publishers. Such names as Dragon's Dream and Visions. She still had Patrick Woodrufffe's intricate work and Mouse and Kelly's record sleeve book. She often looked at the design reading 'American Beauty' or 'American Reality', depending on how you viewed it. Were they still producing these things? The fashion for fantasy seemed to have gone. Now, in the mid Eighties, records had given way to tape. Turning a corner she saw a book on optics. Riveted by its info on rainbows, moonbows and other mysteries, she bought it and returned to Hanover Square.

On approaching the square, an old wino in a filthy mac, hair cropped in a short back and sides, stood waving his bottle in the middle of the road. He muttered angrily to himself or anyone around. The square had recently been landscaped, with new seats, railings and gates. On passing one of the seats, Cath noticed a shaven headed youth. He wiped his eyes with the back of his hand. A tear rolled down his cheek.

Part 4

Chapter 16

Cath had awakened early, but asthma had slowed her down. Lateness for work threatened. Passing one of the larger villas on her way, she hid her surprise at what she saw in its garden. A dark faced figure stood with spreading hands, as if to catch the heavy rain, splashing from leaf to leaf. His expression was of rapture, though his grey suit looked soaked. As she hurried on, she recalled a conversation with her cousin.

'I hear you've got Indian neighbours now' said Brenda.

'Yes.' said Cath 'I saw the women sitting cross-legged on the lawn the other day. It looked just like a scene from one of their paintings!'

Then Brenda told her 'That's not all though. I'm glad you're supporting them, because the former owner had got a black eye from a neighbour at the local Conservative club.'

'You've sold your house to a bunch of bloody wogs!' had accompanied the blow.

Cath was late for work that morning. Sliding quietly into her seat, she hoped to be unnoticed. The room was buzzing with talk of Anne's wedding, the date now finally fixed. Vivien, resourceful as ever, had thought of a way to get money for some earrings she fancied. Producing a part used bottle of Camp coffee, she filled it up with water.

'I'll take it back' she said 'they'll never know the difference!' She smiled, placing it in her shopping bag until lunch time.

Soon afterwards, the sour face of Chapman appeared round the door. He summoned Cath to de Jardin's office. Her heart raced as she dragged herself down the dark stairs.

'Business ees business.' de Jardin began. 'Ze girls do six colourings a day. All except you, so I'm afraid you must go. I'm sorry.'

Curtly, he waved her away. Cath slumped out, sickened, angry. She had

tried so hard and so uselessly. Catching her up on the stairs, the great man's secretary told her
'You can leave at lunch time, with a fortnight's wages.'
Cath accepted, stifling brimming tears.

After lunch, she packed up her belongings and left. She was scarcely missed, in the laughter at Vivien's success with the watered down coffee.
'What a cheek!'
'Try robbing a bank!', they called.
Cath bought a paper and found a seat in Piccadilly gardens. Fresh from the earlier rains, the spring leaves were bright, but she scarcely saw them, or the dressed windows of familiar stores. Scanning the ads, she knew she must get work while her cards were stamped. She was interviewed for a tracing job in a drawing office and asked to start the next Monday.

On the Saturday, the Eighteen Plus crowd went to what seemed an innocuous venue. A dancing school, it held weekly dances. She wore a home sewn dress, in black and white gingham, with detachable skirt. Sitting among the group, on the hard chairs fringing the room, she wasn't so conscious of the more youthful dancers. Her thoughts wandered to the previous day. Remembering Anne's recent marriage, she had carefully chosen an expensive table cloth and taken it to de Jardin's. She wished she hadn't wasted her money. Ann merely looked embarrassed. Before she could thank Cath, the studio manager dashed in.
'You don't work here any more. Now get out!' he shouted. 'and don't let me see you here again.'

Tears started to Cath's eyes at the memory, but she dashed them away, as a tall figure approached. A lean strong face bent close, asking for a dance. There was something strange about his eyes, but his Scottish accent attracted.
'What part of Scotland are you from?' Cath asked.
'Skye' he answered, without enthusiasm.
'That sounds lovely!' she went on, but he cut short her image of mountains and sea with his curt
'You're sentimental, aren't you?'

Though annoyed, she thought 'He's right!' She should know better, after the wedding present fiasco.

'He'd suit me better than most.' she decided, as they arranged to meet on the Sunday.

They met in a local pub, where he spoke vaguely of a bookbinding job. He looked stiff and uneasy in the comfortable lounge. She told him about her problems jobwise.

He countered, 'I was a psychiatric nurse for years.'

He plunged into a diatribe on psychotic patients. It didn't seem genuine somehow. Her misgivings grew as he went for more drinks. Though thin, his shoulders looked huge below his short haircut.

Even so, she wasn't prepared for what happened next. After more drinks, they left the pub, only streets from her cousin's. Passing a gate in a high stone wall, the Scotsman pushed Cath inside among rank smelling weeds. Without word or smile, he thrust his penis into her hand. Drawing away, she was flung to the ground. He was kneeling astride her, sinewy hands on her throat. Spitting in her face, he hissed

'Little bitch little bitch!'

She struggled to free herself, through a sense of paralysis. As his strong grip tightened, her legs had been pushing with all their strength. To her sudden surprise, he keeled over backwards with a groan. She was on her feet, flying across the road without looking. Tears of relief sprang to her eyes, as a couple at the familiar bus stop reached out comforting hands. Astounded, they saw an umbrella clatter into the road and a handbag soar over the high stone wall. A tall figure sped away, coat flying Dracula like behind.

They walked with Cath to her cousin's, where Brenda called the police. With little sympathy, one officer remarked

'We get a lot of this sort of thing.'

The other added 'You can't blame the men when the women lead them on. If you see him again, give us a call.'

Nodding curtly to Cath, the pair left. For months, she dreaded seeing the high walled garden, with its overhanging trees. But she forced herself to pass it and the fear gradually lessened.

Cath wasn't looking forward to the drawing office. More humiliation, more starting afresh. Would her control snap, in a temper over some trifle? Was she being paranoid? 'I'll have to knuckle under.' she thought, 'At least it pays more money. Pushing thirty, now calling herself Miss Hunt, from tart she was now seen as spinster. The latest jokes went minus their punch lines when she was around. Week after week, tracing over meaningless machine parts, their names were often a source of amusement. So often they had a sexual slant, 'bolt nipple' or 'ball cock'.

Joining the union brought a copy of its magazine. After the letters, Cath was faced with the 'Tracers' Page'. Assumed to be political morons, their page featured knitting patterns and household hints. Her letter of complaint went unprinted. Still, she accepted a lift to a union weekend school.

At six a.m. that Saturday morning, the lamplight paled in a rosy dawn. From her cousin's doorway to the gate seemed endless, as Cath teetered towards the cars, the focus of many eyes.

'Widow, divorced or something?' she caught from the back seat, as she climbed into the front, to the right of the driver.

'How do you like the Nash Rambler?' asked another voice.

'Great.' Cath answered, though in ignorance – waiting in bus queues was more in her line. The much admired car was American, she gathered. A peripheral glance at the driver showed glossy dark hair. As he let the wheel sinuously slide through his fingers, excitement chased envy of a possible wife.

Around eleven, they arrived at their hotel, near Blackpool. It stood back from the road, behind a full car park. Solidly square, its white surface needed a repaint. A chill wind blew as they left the cars. Inside, its red carpet promised warmth. After coffee and a tedious preamble, Cath turned at an exciting touch. Glancing down was Alan, the paragon of the Nash Rambler.

'We're going to the Winter Gardens tonight. You coming?' he asked, olive eyes searching her own.

'I'd love to!' she agreed.

Entering the ballroom, it was a change to be swept right away among the dancers. A faceted spotlight winked among trellised plants, picking out Brylcremed heads. Whirling in a quick waltz past anxious eyed girls, Cath felt one of the lucky ones. 'Don't get sentimental!' she told herself, wary of a possible let down. They danced on, as quickstep followed waltz. Newly washed hair flopped over Alan's face. His cavalry twill suit and regimental tie were different. As they sat out for drinks, an ancient Wurlitzer mushroomed from the floor, its player in white tie and tails.

Not all the members were around for the heavy breakfast, but there was no way Cath was going to miss it. After coffee, they got down to union business. As brother followed brother, her attention flagged. She thought of bringing up the tracer's page, but decided against it. She could imagine the condescending smiles it would provoke. After coffee, Alan drove the group home, arranging to see Cath again. Back at her cousin's, it felt dreary.

Several weeks passed, with cinema visits and an Indian meal. These evenings finished unusually early. Alan then dropped her at her cousin's around ten, saying
'My mother's made soup for me.' or some such.
From worrying about a wife, Cath found herself envying a mother – a new situation so far.

Hearing of the eighteen plus rambles, Alan proposed a hike in the Derbyshire hills. Unable to afford pukkha gear, Cath turned up in her old trench coat and suede winter boots. A grin and raised eyebrows were Alan's only comment, not being much better clad. The early spring morning was bright. A fine drizzle threw a rainbow over their path. Heavy clouds to the west gave way to fleece white, then drifted away. Rain fresh grasses shone bright as limes in the sun. Nearing a wood, the path grew steeper. Cath was soon twenty paces behind. She thought Alan should have slowed down, knowing of her asthma.
'I must have a rest soon Alan.' she insisted. Alan called
'Let's eat up here. The view's great.'

They rested on the low hill, unpacking their food. After more ephedrine, Cath's breathing eased. With a new clarity, a river below, splashed over mossy stones. High after rain, it washed the lower leaves of trees. As they wandered on, the valley darkened below a gilded sky. Unsure of the route, Alan took out his map and decided to head towards Buxton.

Wearily they reached the now darkening town. A hotel, its palatial lawns lit by round arched windows revived Cath's flagging steps. Choosing a more modest hotel for the night, Alan booked single rooms. Awaking next morning around six, chest heaving, Cath had to resort to her tablets. As she drifted to sleep again in starched white sheets, their crocheted edges brought back the past. Lavender polish scented the room. Later, a twist of the doorknob ended her dream, as the drug poured its wild sweetness through her veins. Climbing in beside her, Alan more than fulfilled his earlier promise.

Through the following week, Cath's drawing office days were rich with relived delights. About to meet Alan's mother, she wondered what the matriarch thought of Alan's weekend away. She prepared herself for an ordeal. Their part of the city was new to her. For what seemed hours, the Nash swept through street after hideous street. A bombsite was fringed by terraced rows like open wounds, wallpapers flapping. Around the corner of a co-op, another great flatness loomed, broken by a still standing pub.

Gradually Cath saw a little more green. Market gardens, allotments, then a valley with trees.
'That's Daisy Nook, where I played as a kid', broke in Alan.
'We're here now' he added as he drove past a thirties style terrace.
Distantly, a pithead wheel traced the sky. Alan drew up outside his home, its square bays looking onto a leafy front garden. The door was opened by his mother. Tall and erect, her hand beckoned, its arthritic joints gnarled. An impression of a white perm and glasses.

The talk centred around relatives in London, as tea was poured. Mrs Robb had it appeared, been born on the Old Kent Road, well within the sound of Bow Bells.

'Have you heard from Aunt Do?' Alan asked.

'She rang while you were out.' his mother answered,

'Doris got that job on the BBC phones, starts Monday.'

Her accent was clear enough to Cath. It wasn't so in reverse. Cath's muted tones and his mother's deafness made Alan interpreter. However later, she seemed to hear perfectly.

'You know Cath' Alan went on, 'I was talking to some blokes from the union weekend, the other day. They thought you were about twenty five!'

His mother snapped 'Didn't you ask 'em where they were lookin'?'

Cath merely smiled, though it rankled.

As mother and son reminisced, Cath's eyes scanned the room. On the mantle shelf were photos of uniformed soldiers. One had two stripes, one three. They had to be Alan's brothers, killed in the war. Then she noticed a pathway of carpet pieces stretching from kitchen to fire. It almost covered the large carpet square. 'What was the point' Cath thought, 'of keeping the carpet clean, if even guests couldn't see it?'

A meal of bacon, eggs and tomatoes was followed by a fruit cake. Alan's mother refused the desert.

'I never could abide currants,' she said, then

'as a girl, I never had nothing to eat on a Friday. I'll tell you why.' She smiled grimly and carried on

'My Dad was out of work you see and my mother's wages ran out on a Friday. All we had to eat was a great spotted dick, full of currants that I couldn't eat!' She finished, jaw set, cheeks an angry red.

Chapter 17

A few weeks later, Alan produced a ring in a Thirties setting, turning it to catch the light. Five large diamonds blazed in spectral purity. Cath loved the ring, but hearing it was the remnant of a neighbour's old romance, she refused it. She couldn't forget the 'Opals for Tears' of her first engagement. Instead, clad in a new tight skirted dress, she joined Alan to look for a more ordinary ring. They chose one with five small diamonds embedded in a rectangular frame.

The couple began looking at houses, having fixed on an August wedding. Cath, with her annual money from Huddersfield, bought a handbag, shoes and materials for honeymoon dresses, through spring and then summer. Rural drives, rowing boats on rivers, and evenings in quiet country pubs passed in a dreamlike succession.

As at her first marriage, Cath wore no diaphanous white, but she was thrilled as any virgin.

Her brother's 'We'd all like two lots of presents!' didn't dim her joy.

'Well at least Cath didn't get a fully furnished house!' Bonnie added, with a glance at Lulu.

Her elder sister's wedding gifts from Grandma still rankled.

Lulu cut in 'There was money around then and, if you remember, I was the first to get married.'

'I could be excused for forgetting. There was a war on when I married!', ex Wren Bonnie answered.

'I'm so glad for you. At least one of us two managed it.' Cora smiled, looking very frail.

In their colourful photos, Alan's worry about the future was plain. The simple chapel service was in contrast to Cath's earlier wedding, with stained glass and choir boys. The reception was even simpler, as they sat down to a cold ham salad. The two mothers talked, polite but distant. Later at Lulu's, the couple opened presents. Cath's mother drew her aside to give her an envelope. In it was a cheque for two thousand pounds.

Osbert had finally sold the old shops. It sounded an enormous sum to Cath. She'd surprise Alan later with the news.

At last the couple climbed into the car and drove off. Out of sight, they ditched the tin cans which Osbert had tied on behind. The sun was an excuse to show off the convertible roof. As Cath gave him the news of the windfall, Alan speeded up, shouting

'I love you I love you!'

Reaching the outskirts of Harrogate, he remembered contraceptives. After an embarrassing tour of closed barber's shops, he finally found a supply.

A real coal fire warmed their hotel room. Though welcome, it was little needed..... Next morning they went on to Edinburgh. They booked for the Tattoo that night and for the Kathakali Indian dancers later in the week. Alan, bright eyed, enthused on the regimental bands, the competing, the panache. While not looking forward much to the event, Cath caught the frenzy of the crowd. Fortified by ephedrine for the climb to the citadel, she soon felt its high excitement. In mathematical precision, parade followed gymnast. Human and equine forms coalesced into a brilliance of scarlet and gold, flashing below deepening blue. As they returned to their rooms, a carnival splendour processioned Cath's inner eye. Alan seemed haloed to her. Though still bathed in the glow next day, she now saw blood beneath scarlet, patriarchy implicit in helmet and plume. She recalled the sad framed faces of the sons on the mantelpiece.

On the day of the Indian performance, Cath's asthma was worse. She had to take more drugs, as they set off. Neither knew what to expect. Alan was indifferent, Cath curious, as they took their seats. Against a black backcloth, a tall youth appeared, transsexual in a white sari. He danced barefoot, to music of a strange beauty. As the drama unfolded, the insistent beat of the drum became one with Cath's heightened heartbeat. Figures, demoniacally masked and haloed, projected a fearful frenzied joy. Ankle bells gleamed below their wide white skirts. High hats were tier on tier like pagodas, haloes behind. Cath remembered de Quincey on opium, how roofs repeated to incredible heights. She had read how a prince's first sight of the Portuguese had inspired the costumes Under the influence of the poppy, Cath supposed. ... As music and dance flowed on, Alan's head drooped on her shoulder and he slept. It seemed incredible to her that he could sleep through the thrilling performance.

Drives through the countryside, cafes, hotels merged in memory as the honeymoon ended. Then the couple moved to their new house, with picture windows and L shaped room. Cath didn't miss her cousin's drab home. With some of the windfall, they bought a four seater sofa with a matching armchair, and teak furniture, with a low hanging lamp over the dining table. Scatter cushions in the peacock lemon and greens of the curtains delighted Cath. Not so Alan.

'That's for puffs!' he sneered, when she tried to whip up his enthusiasm.

Alan's mother came to tea the next Sunday. Cath had prepared a great spread. She had put a special effort into the coffee cake, made with brown sugar and walnut icing. Cath kept her cool, but only just, when the old lady remarked, smiling sweetly,

'Is it a Mary Baker?'

The mother having got in her dig, the rest of the evening passed off uneventfully.

As the months passed, Cath saw a difference in their love. Alan had a decency, a restraint, foreign to Cath. Sometimes his coolness chilled. To a kiss on the back of his neck at breakfast, he hissed

'There's a time and place for everything.'

Before long, Cath found herself pregnant. She carried on working until the last two months.
You want to give up now and let Alan earn the money.'
The draughtsmen hinted, but she wanted to earn as long as she could. She would miss the company, though she hadn't got too friendly with the tracers, all around nineteen or twenty.

Cath had a long labour, thirty-six hours. At first, she wondered what the fuss was about. In her hospital room, she read Frazer's 'Golden Bough'. An anthropological tome full of navel strings and fertility rites, it was hardly a good choice. Faint cries, sounds of vomiting with a nurse's reproof, drifted from a nearby ward. For a day and a half Cath's contractions were weak. Then, heavily drugged, she dreamed of a fire engine's scream and awoke to incredible pain. Gritting her teeth, she stared fixedly at a mark on the wall. 'I won't scream the place down, like women on TV.' she resolved, keeping it up through the hell. With a dreamlike image of a ball being pushed through a hole, she knew delivery was near.

When wheeled into the labour ward, a nurse ordered
'Count up to ten!'
Hazy with drugs, only the woman's mounting urgency forced Cath to comply. Finally crying out as flesh tore, her girl baby was born. Seeing the little face, so like her own, she felt instant love. Later Alan came in jauntily, dropping a bunch of flowers on her bed.
'One of the inferior sex is it?' he smiled.
White faced, hair dank with sweat, Cath stared with blood shot eyes, hating him at that moment.

The little house seemed idyllic, when Cath came home with infant Vanessa. In spite of Alan's flippancy, his constant caring surprised Cath. When the baby cried at night, he leapt out of bed before Cath had opened an eye. A health visitor arrived next day.
'A normal housewife.' she murmured, ticking off Cath's name on her list.
This amused Cath, who had never felt normal in her life. Noticing Cath's wheezing, the health visitor suggested a cleaner.
'My husband wouldn't wear that!' Cath commented.
'Well he should, you could get a home help.' she went on.
'Oh no! I'm not an invalid!' Cath exclaimed, but she knew her asthma was worse.

Her tablets were now three, three times a day. One morning they weren't working and each breath was hell. She scraped up a sandwich while Vanessa slept, took extra tablets and began to eat. A Brandenburg Concerto began on the radio. The drugs at last brought relief. She closed her eyes to savour each now crystalline note. On a velvet darkness bright paisleys floated in stately procession, in time to the bass. Within them, smaller ones flashed iridescent, to violin or flute. An ecstasy reigned over all....

Unbearably, the music ended and boring normality returned. Still vivid, Cath recalled the varied shapes, each with its border of dots or squares. They were so like the textile paisleys, it could be no accident. Tedious as they had been to paint, she could see their origins now. So much for the so called Indian 'pine', on the old calicos.

Later, Cath took a spade into the garden and altered the shape of an oval bed. A paisley now surrounded the rose bush, a reminder of the morning's experience! Ill from the exhaustion, she rang for a visit from her GP. On his way out, Dr Montgomery pointed with his umbrella to the new garden bed, commenting

'Was this in memory of your textile design work?'

He bent to look at her closely as he spoke, adding

'I know you wouldn't abuse the tablets Catherine.'

One Sunday afternoon, Cath's brother and his wife arrived unexpectedly. Their serious air unnerved Cath, as she got out cups and made tea. 'Is it Cora?' she thought, then Osbert began

'We've some bad news Love.' He faltered and Rita finished

'Your mother's had a heart attack.'

Cath broke into tears. She hadn't seen her mother for months and they'd been distant. Now they could never get closer.... Her twin Cora had been living with their mother, in the flat Cath had once shared with Basil.

'What will Cora do? Can she manage on her own?' Cath asked.

'We'll work something out.' Osbert answered and Rita added

'She won't go into a nunnery anyway, she applied, but they wouldn't take her! Apparently nuns must be fit as fleas! Even a Cheshire Home wouldn't have her, poor lass. She's terminally ill now you know.'

Cath hadn't known. It added to the shock. Rita carried on 'Lulu and I thought of having her for three months alternately. Would you take a turn as well?'

Cath accepted, though she saw that Alan looked dubious.

Cora soon arrived for her three months stay. Weighing six stone to Cath's eight, the twins were far from identical now. It was hard to remember how close they'd once been, knowing even their thoughts were the same. Could she ever be so close in thought to Alan? She doubted it. He resented that the threesome was now a foursome.

'We might as well have Ma here, if we can't be on our own.' he complained.

Finding Cora crying in her room one morning, Cath felt powerless to comfort or help.

'Jesus, help me!' Cora cried.

Tears were streaming through sodden tissues, forming rivulets down her emaciated arms Cath wanted to keep her there, feed her up, give her some hope, but she could see Alan's irritation. She didn't have the courage to risk her new life, fragile and ephemeral as it seemed. Cora stayed for three months, then moved to Lulu's at Huddersfield. Her health rapidly worsening, she went into hospital, weighing only three stones.

She later transferred to a nursing home, where Cath took Vanessa to see her.

'At least one of us has managed to reproduce.' Cora smiled, as Vanessa, on her bed, emptied the meagre contents of her handbag.

The child's alert face contrasted with the somnolent ones, half hidden beneath covers on the neighbouring beds. Eyes glazed, mouths half open, they already appeared dead. To see Cora in this place, dying before her time, pierced Cath with grief and guilt. Cora opened the present Cath had brought her.

'Thanks,' she said 'but I don't think I'll ever wear it....'

She pushed the sweater on one side despairingly.

A few months later Cora died at the home.

'Just room for one more.'

Osbert said of the grave, its headstone put up at their grandfather's death. In granite, it was modest among Victorian marbles nearby. One mill owner's tomb towered over others, its bland angel spreading great wings. As Cora's small coffin was lowered into the grave, tears came. The voice of the priest, the wind, the rain and the blurring Autumn leaves faded. Cath saw the sun drenched walks to school, the wanderings through Layton Fields.... She recalled a priest at another grave, on their first school days. Cora had seemed enthralled....

As the family group lingered, Cath turned to see the priest beckoning. His cassock billowed in the wind that carpeted the graves with leaves.

'Your sister had a very happy death,' he said to Cath as he took her aside.

He told how Cora had died peacefully on one of his visits. He felt it would comfort her to know. Thanking him, she joined the family, though in her thoughts still far off in their childhood in Huddersfield.

Cath returned to Manchester and the present. She threw herself into friendship with neighbours. Joyce, the young mother next door, had a similar age daughter. Plump and rosy like her mother, the child marched in as if owning the place. Whenever Vanessa got a toy from her basket, little Mandy snatched it away. Soon she was almost buried in a mountain of toys. Her fat little face looked out triumphantly, podgy hands poised to take more. While Joyce drank coffee, smiling her approval, Cath seethed. Vanessa, stoically toyless, made no attempt to regain any of her things. Finally disengaged from the pile, Mandy strode out, her oversized head with its ponytail reminiscent of the widowed Queen Victoria.

A year later, Cath became pregnant again. On her visits to Doctor Montgomery for check-ups, she would get more than a verbal response. His hot hand would linger on thigh or breast. 'It's because he knows about the ephedrine, or is he known for it?' she thought, I'll have a word with Joyce.' When Cath broached the subject after coffee, Joyce laughed, blushing.

'I had trouble getting pregnant with Mandy,' she said, 'when he carried on like that, I thought he was testing for frigidity! I know now he tries it on every woman.'

Cath hadn't the courage to put a stop to the doctor's liberties. His heavy browed face recalled her father. When Alan's mother visited, it was more embarrassing still.

'Come in Sir.' she smiled, as she let the GP in.

Her Army wife's subservience was anathema to Cath. Entering the front room, the doctor enquired 'And how are the breasts?', the heat of his touch searing through the flesh. Though her back was towards the old lady, Cath was sure she had seen. They never spoke of the matter.

However, her mother-in-law proved priceless when Cath was in labour. Heavy with drugs, she could hear as in a dream, the distant voice of the midwife.

'Look at that for relaxation! There was nothing like that in our day, was there?'

'You're right there,' Mrs Robb agreed,

'I had three of 'em!'

So complete was the relaxation, that Cath couldn't respond to the faint sounding voice. As the midwife smothered her in oil, her rising shrillness finally broke through. Supported by Alan's mother, Cath gave birth to a boy.

The tiny infant, with its mop of black hair was named Mark. Vanessa, brought to Cath's bed by her grandmother, now seemed huge. At two, she stood up better to next door Mandy. Joyce too had had a son. Like his sister, he wasn't a willing sharer. Later, looking from the kitchen window, it angered Cath to see little Roy rush in, grabbing Mark's tractor right away. Mark would climb onto Roy's old tricycle, rather than risk losing his friend.

One cold November morning, as the sun broke through the mist, Cath planned a garden clear up, while Vanessa played next door. Mark sat on his tractor in his fur hooded suit, not pedalling around as usual. His eyes looked unnaturally bright, but Cath hardly noticed, hacking away at straggling branches. At lunch time, she saw with a start that the tractor was still. Mark was asleep, slumped over its wheel. Pushing back his hood to feel his forehead, Cath saw that his cheeks were a fiery red. Her cold hand awoke him and he stared with strangely bright eyes, then sank back into sleep.

Rushing him inside, she rang for any available doctor, hoping not to see the harassing Montgomery. She made Mark a bed on the sofa, banked up the fire and waited. Though it was Montgomery, she was glad to see him. He walked in, stethoscope in hand, but a glance at the child sent him back to his car. Using a strange looking stethoscope, he announced

'I'm afraid Mark has a meningism.'

Cath's heart raced at the word, so like meningitis. Grabbing a pad, she wrote down the GP's advice. He promised to visit next morning.

Alan arrived home to the shock of seeing a changeling. The plucking of tiny hands at the bed clothes and the unresponsive gaze of dilate eyes brought an unspoken dread. Vanessa in bed, the parents spent the evening and then the night, cooling the hot little body with cloths. Dr. Montgomery called in the morning.

'He'll have to go in I'm afraid.' he told Cath.

Neighbours took in Vanessa, as Cath followed the small stretcher into the ambulance. She couldn't restrain tears at the hospital, when she saw Mark in a machine, naked under glass like a specimen in a jar. A lumbar puncture confirmed meningitis.

Cath visited the hospital every day, fearing a trauma like she and Cora had gone through. Alan's mother, now Grandma, looked after Vanessa. Cath saw that other children weren't so lucky. The child in the next bed cried continuously. Getting no response, she gradually lapsed into silence, hardly responding when her parents came. Mark soon rallied and was sitting up, playing with his toys. The staff questioned his limited word power of 'teddy' and 'no'. When Cath explained that this was all he could say before coming, they reassured her he didn't have brain damage. When he turned a toy tennis racket into a guitar, to soundlessly accompany the Beatles, Cath knew she didn't have to worry.

Chapter 18

'She's kicking me!' grizzled four year old Mark, waking in the back seat of the car.

'He kicked me first!' Vanessa countered.

They'd been trying to sleep head to toe through the night.

'Bloody well be quiet you two!', Alan hissed. 'How can I drive with that racket going on?'

He'd driven all night and Cath knew he was wishing they'd had an overnight stop. They were on their way to a camping holiday in the French Valley of the Loire. They breakfasted on salty bacon and half-cooked eggs. After the ferry crossing, they hoped to reach their campsite before dusk.

'It must be over an hour since you said we'd be there in half an hour.'

Alan didn't answer. Cath was sure he was lost, as he stopped in a lay-by to look at his map. Driving on past darkening trees, they saw many camp signs, but never their own. When they finally arrived, it was too late to erect their tent. They were forced to spend the night in their car, trying to get some sleep. Next morning, Alan put up the tent in his quick efficient way.

'Don't bother,' he answered when Cath offered help,

'I'll get it done quicker on my own!'

Exhausted with driving, he spent the afternoon asleep in the Anglia, after dropping off the family at the chateau of Azay le Rideau. Looking back as he settled into sleep, Cath was stirred at the sight of him, the lock of hair slipping over one eye, the dark lashes on his cheek.

Alan's words echoed in Cath's mind as she and the children took the dusty path to the chateau. He had called to mind first husband Basil, when he remarked

'These bastards have milked generations of peasants to build these monstrosities!'

He was oblivious to the perfection that remained when courtiers and kings had gone.

Disappointment at his viewpoint vanished when, rounding a corner, the chateau appeared. Every rich delight of its surface was twinned in its moat's bright water. Each conical tower, each roof, each window frame appealed. Why had it this strange familiarity? Then she recalled its miniatures, the homes of the mill owners, lining the new South Road of her youth... . Though these glowed in memory, they seemed mere reflections of an ideal here perfectly expressed. Her excitement grew, as each new vista, seen along the dusty drive, called to mind the old forbidden pathways. Shrouded in leaves of more delicate green, she had glimpsed spires, cupolas, or an oriel window, bright through a deepening mist. Though lesser, they were woven into the fabric of her being, as the French scenes could never be. Through the week, Cath and the children saw many Loire castles, Alan sometimes going with them.

Their final visit was to Chenonceau, just Cath and the children. A breeze scattered rose petals, scenting the air as they passed. The pale chateau had an ethereal calm. On the far bank, its spires and turrets reached for the bland sky. Lower rooms rose over a many arched bridge. Seeing the dual image in the flowing Cher, Cath loved its strange asymmetry. Could it be incomplete? she thought. Looking back, she noticed a solitary male, passing through the gardens with a rapt expression. They did exist then, men who felt as she did. Men were after all the creators of these scenes. A desolation possessed her, as they walked through the echoing rooms.

They spent the next week by the sea. The children took on a new life with Alan, swimming, ball games and sand castles. Their long limbs flew across the sands, sun bleached hair, a lime bikini. Cath tried swimming, until the chill of the sea brought on asthma. Fragmentary impressions of turreted roofscapes lingered in memory. She idly experimented with water ribbed sand. Running it through her fingers, it formed ethereal and delicate peaks. On outcrops of rock, she began to create chateaux, spired and towered with mossy green lawns. Around them were seaweed trees, far below, lapping shores. As she worked, she conceived new paintings. She was eager to begin them at home.

On their return, Mark started school. Walking down the steep hill, Cath wanted to hold his hand but refrained. With Vanessa and the neighbouring children, he went in without a backward glance. Relieved, she bought brushes and the new acrylic paint, paying from their joint account. Excitedly, she began work. She drew on the canvas with ruler and compass. Through precision she aimed for a dream like ambience, as in the chateaux themselves. Strange facades would surround a square, the lower ones like reflections. A machicolated tower, an oriel window, would appear in magenta, turquoise or lime. Paisley like dots or squares would edge each unreal tree, as patterned windows stared.

At times Cath felt the work to be futile, a mere talking to herself. What outlet could she ever hope to find for it?. Still she carried on. It gave meaning to her now solitary days, was something to look forward to between chores. The first painting finished, she began on another, this time in orange, reds and red purples. Catching the light, gold glinted. Buildings rose around a triangle. Geometric patterns formed windows and paved a mosaic like surround. Enthusiasm waxing, she worked on in the evening, on the rare nights when Alan was out. She had difficulty in getting the children to settle. They would demand story after story, aware that her mind was elsewhere.

Alan's mother now came round every Thursday afternoon. Her son took her home around ten. Today as usual, the old lady grasped her cup of tea with the eagerness of the fully addicted. For the umpteenth time, Cath listened to the annoying monologue.

'I had a good 'usband, my dear. Regular as clockwork on a Friday, he gave me his wage packet unopened and waited for me to give him his spends!'

A lecture on household management was next; on how to find the shops where each item was cheapest, sugar at the Co-op, bacon in the town.

'Look after the pennies and the pounds will look after themselves.' she cliched.

Cath privately thought that if you looked after the pounds, the pennies would look after themselves, but she had little opportunity to put it into practice these days. When she'd used up her cheque book for their joint account, another book wasn't forthcoming. Alan thought it better that they only had one book, his! He could keep better track of the money, he explained. She could always ask if there was anything she wanted. Asking might not be getting, she thought. She knew that her artistic outgoings were the cause of his worry. She resented the web she was caught in, but what could she do? His canny old mother had been far better off! Cath pushed away thoughts of her own mother's dependence.

Later over a second cup of tea, the matriarch enthused on 'silent temper.' By this she had controlled her husband, not speaking to him for weeks at a time, if he displeased her.

'That way, I 'ad the upper 'and, you see!' she finished, eyes gleaming.

Cath slipped out to fetch the children from school, glad of the relief from the grandmother's never ending monologue.

After completing her two new paintings, Cath planned to take them to the local galleries and see what reaction they produced. In newly pressed flairs, waist long hair in a bun, she set off. Tentatively, she entered the older establishment. Undoing brown paper wrappings, her heart thumped. She placed her work on the counter, to be told

'These aren't really paintings my dear. They're more like tea towel designs. I'm sorry.'

Embarrassed Cath rushed from the scene, tearing the paper as she hastened to repack.

The second gallery, scorning the competent landscapes of the first, showed abstracts reminiscent of Rothko et al. These were huge, arranged sparsely in two white rooms. Still more daunted, Cath repeated her spiel. She hurried out almost before hearing the verdict.

'Not what we're looking for.' smiled the long haired assistant.

It was small consolation that the place soon closed. There'd been little support from the locals.

By then, Cath had embarked on an ambitious new project. Though the mystic scenes meant a lot to her, they seemed futile without gallery response. To find out what was going on in the art world, she subscribed to a year's supply of 'Studio International'. Named from the Victorian 'Studio', a lily leafed decadence survived on its cover. Not so inside. Cath became enthused by its reviews of the latest extremes. She decided to aim upmarket, spurred on by an irrational hope.

The children left for school muffled up these cold mornings.

'Put your masks on if it's foggy.' Cath told them, suspecting they wouldn't.

She knew they would cast off some item round the corner, but she couldn't live their lives for them. She waved and closed the door, eyes bright with her self-imposed task. After a trial with brush and acrylic, she had bought an air-brush and compressor. Alan paid for it reluctantly, from the so called joint account.

Cath was working on a series of twelve inch triangles. Miniature triangles covered each surface, in close gradations of colour. Nine triangles would form a large one, its corners magenta, vermilion and ruby. Her aim was a great array of these shapes. Graduating from one spectral hue to another, they would come full circle to magenta. They could combine to form chevrons, hexagons and large triangles. Cath didn't worry about galleries, that could come later.

Yet another Christmas Day had arrived. The turkey, at last in the oven, was packed with its forcemeat and stuffing. Cath poured herself a sherry, hoping to see the Beatles' TV show, before her mother-in-law's arrival. As the Magical Mystery Tour unfolded, Cath was lost in its world. Then the doorbell rang.

'Daddy's brought Grandma!' Vanessa enthused, fond as she was of that lady.

She rushed to the door as Cath trailed behind, straining to catch the faint notes, lest the magic fade. Handing out sherry and cake, Cath tried to show interest, but eye and ear were drawn to the screen. The displeased matriarch lapsed into silence, broken by the metronome click of her dentures, an additional beat to that of the Four.

Later, the main course over, they lingered over pudding and rum sauce. The exceptions were Mark and his grandmother. Cath had baked them a special cake as they hated dried fruit. It was fruitless but royally iced. Thus pacified, the old lady was speaking again. She was to stay for a week with the family.

A curious phenomenon of the holiday was Alan's desire for love. Bright eyed and eager, his usual reticence seemed gone, while his mother remained in the house. Was there some Oedipal connection? Cath probed no further, simply enjoying the change.

Vanessa and Mark played with dolls and Action men, when not glued to TV. The action men partnered Barbie and Cindy, in the Christmas Cindy car and jeep. They careered around the floor, ending at a wild party in the doll's house. The wine and chocolate filled days sped by. Turkey and chips followed turkey and salad, until curry and goulash finished the bird off. Taking the last of the fruit-free cake, the mother-in-law finally departed.

Winter warming into Spring, the family had walks and drives at weekends. One Sunday they collected white spreading blossoms, for Alan's elderflower wine. Fiddling with filters and jars, he filled the house with the richest of scents. Cath thought of the evenings alone in bed sitters, seeming so far away now.

These idyllic days were not to last, redundancies loomed. Though a senior draughtsman, Alan was among those affected. As his three month's notice neared its end, the signs of his depression were familiar to Cath. Lingering at table after meals with a glazed look, he was irritable at the least distraction. The three months up, no job was in sight. Politically, he swerved further to the left.

As he sat around filling in job applications, Cath put away her triangular art. Concentration was now impossible. More painful was the effect on the children. Shamefaced, they collected their free school meals. Now also scanning the situations vacant, an advert caught Cath's eye. It read.
'Artist wanted, for temporary work.'
She got the job, though it was only for a fortnight, with another fortnight a month or two later. It was promotion work at Rushforth's store,

for Azdec products for men.

The store had an air of quiet bustle, when Cath arrived before nine. A blonde assistant in a mini-skirted outfit was dusting the perfumery counter.

'Danny, the barber, isn't here yet.' she explained, pulling up a chair.

With a back stage excitement Cath took in the glow of mirrored lamps, the colourful displays. Staff dragged in a large barber's chair, attempting to blow away dust. Its chromium arms placed it thirty years earlier.

'You can get rid of that!' cried the barber, just arriving, as he fingered the lingering dust.

To Cath, his heavy brows recalled her father, but he relaxed into a smile.

Her role became clear when he brought out chairs, a new barber's chair and one for herself. Getting out her sketch pad and pencil, Cath watched as the promotional team got to work, all in the lemon mini outfits. The brunette, tall and confident on her five inch heels, grabbed a microphone and began

'Come along fellers!. Get your Azdec, created for men with women in mind!'

Attracted by the glittering products displayed by the girls, a youth was persuaded into the waiting seat. As the barber Danny combed short locks into Beatle like fullness, Cath sketched the final effect, taking ten minutes or so. A crowd gathered and the girls circulated, pressing their wares on the less resisting. Such was the Azdec promotion.

Cath spoke little at coffee and lunch, not feeling quite one of the girls, but she really enjoyed the first day. Though stressed about Alan, she loved the clamour, the excitement, the brilliance of lamps mirrored among avenues of gifts.

Most sitters looked pleased with their portraits. If not, they didn't comment. A good looking Indian asked why she'd made him so white. Not sure herself, she told him 'I thought

'I'd lose the contrast, if I piled on the pencil.'

He smiled as he put the sketch in his briefcase. She felt more than annoyed when a male voice from the crowd remarked

'You shouldn't be doing this!. You're taking away a man's livelihood.'

'If I can do the job, why shouldn't I get paid for it?' she answered, to murmured approval from some.

A younger man, apparently in advertising, offered advice on a slick commercial style. Ignoring him, she carried on as before. Raising his hand to comb another sitter, Danny suddenly hissed

'Get out and don't come back until your head's clean!'

The man crept silently away, scratching his head.

'Danny's got style.' the promotion girls whispered, as he flashed his mirror and comb.

'Cath deserves the accolades.' was the general manager's verdict.

At the end of the fortnight, she got twice what she'd asked for. Should she have asked for more?

Eventually, Alan's persistence paid off. A job as chief draughtsman would entail moving south. Cath's second promotion being in Liverpool, it seemed an excuse for a holiday using their caravan, which they had acquired after their trip to the Loire. They parked the caravan on a coastal site, where pines ran down to the shore. As Alan drove her to the store, Cath hoped he would cope with the children all day.

She entered the new store, alert, excited. Again the glamour and glitter were there. Coming in from the bright sun, rainbow tones spot lit the darker space.

'Hello Love!' called Danny, arranging their chairs.

A new set of women, in the same mini uniforms, paused in their chatting as he introduced her. They spread around with their gift packs and a crowd soon gathered.

'See how you'd look with a Beatle cut.' smiled Danny.

The Azdec promotion was underway.

On the Tuesday, Alan told Cath

'I've planned a swimming pool session for today, the kids are bored with the campsite.'

Waiting at the store that evening, a shame-faced Alan arrived with

Mark. Explaining

'Vanessa's at the dental hospital.',

he described the disastrous day.

'I was with Mark at the shallow end, taking my eyes off Vanessa for seconds. Climbing out, she slipped, smashing her teeth on the edge!'

Cath pictured the scene. Blood streaking the water! A tidal wave rocking the pool, as Alan vaulting the steps, gathered up Vanessa, a startled Mark under his arm.

Guilt smote Cath, when Vanessa smiled bravely, her protruding front teeth now two jagged stumps. Always problematic, the teeth had caused endless visits to the dentists and wearing of a brace. Cath heard that an orthodontist could cap them at sixteen, but it would seem an eternity to the nine year old.

Too soon for Cath, the promotion was over. She was back home, with little to do but the housework. Some months later, the family set off on the long drive south. Alan feared their investment there was anything but sound. Known as 'the Coach House' the property was originally a stable block. It had belonged to a great Gothic hall, now in flats. They had a view across gardens of its pinnacled roofs. Well designed details hid what Alan saw as virtually a wreck. Persuaded by Cath, he had decided to buy, to free his mind for priorities. The new job needed full concentration. Cath hoped that the move would create opportunities for her.

As they neared the West Sussex town, it seemed a new world, yet strangely familiar. The Tudor farms and thatch roofed cottages seemed cloyingly sweet as the boxes of chocolates they recalled. Could Cath fit into this cosiness, or did she want to? She cut short her reverie, as she saw gleaming white gates, fronting a courtyard. Stepping from the car, a rich perfume disarmed her. Flowering creepers climbed the crumbling brickwork, adding an enchantment to the extended walls. Their starkness was muted only by stable windows.

The family entered the new home, to a disorder of furniture and tea chests. Cath hurriedly made up the children's bunk beds, in an attic room under the eaves. Mark and Vanessa asleep, she and Alan soon followed, flinging on purple sheets and an Indian red cover.

'Let's leave the mess til tomorrow.' Alan yawned, curling up close.

In the morning Cath, hating the disarray even more than its clearance, soon emptied the tea chests. Alan heaved furniture into place.

By degrees they became aware of the oddities of the house, if such it could be called. The flat roofed kitchen was left of the courtyard. Next was the entrance lobby, its pine floors continuing through the dining room. Up a stairway were their bedroom, en suite bathroom and a sitting room, the stairs carrying on to the attic. To the right was a studio, once a hay loft for stables beneath. These were now garages for the flats in the Victorian house. Still further along was a room they kept locked. Though treated, woodworm had eaten a third of its floor. A great hole yawned like a mouth. Worse was a doorway at the attics far end. This opened onto a platform, high above the studio, a single rail over the drop.

With the children now settled in new schools, Cath turned to the problem of Alan's mother. Alone in Manchester, she might get depressed or senile. On the other hand, Cath couldn't face the thought of her living with them, as Alan would have liked. How could she get any creative work done? She rang Social Services and made an appointment. Setting off, she soon reached a bus stop facing a hospital. The day was warm and patients stood among the trees. Cath watched with a faint chill. One ritually bounced a ball on a string, while some stared into space. A psychiatric hospital on their doorstep? It would have put her off the house, if she'd realised its closeness. She could end up here herself, if she didn't find somewhere for the matriarch.

Through corridors and lifts, Cath finally found the right department. Across his polished desk, a stocky official answered her questions.

'Accommodation's scarce you know. We do have a warden attended flat available, but you must let me know by tomorrow.'

Answering 'We'll contact you.', she hurried into the drenching rain.

Passing the hospital, the odour of overcooked cabbage hung around.

Alan showed no interest in the flat for his mother.

'She'd never come down here, unless it was to live with us'

he said. 'I couldn't even get her into the car!'

'But can't you see?' Cath protested, 'It would solve so many problems. She wouldn't be on top of us, and you and the kids could still see her. We could have her to tea every Sunday, just as we used to do'.

Alan stonewalled, refusing discussion. A later phone call confirmed that the flat had gone.

Chapter 19

Cath booked an orthodontist for Vanessa's teeth, broken at the holiday pool. She accompanied her daughter the first few times, though it wasn't far, mostly through leafy lanes. Vanessa appeared fearless, enjoying the attention, relaxing with magazines among potted palms. Cath later let her go alone. Small streets emerged onto the great highway. Crossing lights, so far distant, were hard to see. Vanessa, tall for her nine years, determinedly crossed the Brighton road.

The jagged teeth could not be capped until growth had slowed, around sixteen. Cath tried to conjure up Vanessa's future. A perfect smile and contact lenses. The metamorphosis seemed unlikely when she looked at the brace and the glasses. She saw a Vanessa in a long dress and hippie beads, forgetting the transience of fashion.

About three one morning, Mark pattered down from his attic room. Curious, Cath followed him into the bathroom. Sounds of splashing came not from the sink but the toilet, where Mark was washing his hands! Cath stared as, towelling his hands, Mark looked through her. Creeping behind, she watched her son climb into bed with a far away gaze.

Cath's thoughts flew to the rail over the studio.
'For God's sake Alan, will you do something about that rail!' she pestered. 'If he's sleepwalking he could be killed any night.'
He promised to fix something up temporarily. Looking at the rail, she was far from reassured. It seemed fragile, and was at least two yards from the ground. She wandered through the bare studio below, still full of earlier occupants' rubbish. She hoped to find some junk that would fill up the gap. Instead, she found what she hadn't expected, a pile of fresh looking animal turds! 'Whatever else!' she thought. Phoning the previous owners, she queried the droppings.
'Guinea pigs!' was the instant reply.
Too instant, Cath thought. They had to be rat turds. A rodent operator came and put poison down, but no animal ate it.

Cath was working again on her triangles project. She placed one of them on a thrown-together bench that ran along the studio wall. In the strong sunlight, its fine gradations of tone were clear. On the still white area, she masked out a small triangle, with the rest covered over. Carefully mixing half and quarter teaspoons with water in the airbrush jar, she began spraying. She sprayed areas on several triangles, each drying as she went on to the next. Now it was lunch time. Leaving the work on the bench, she knocked up a sandwich and coffee.

As she ate, resting her copy of Solzenitzen's 'Closed Circle' against the percolator, she envied the prisoners he described. At least they had company! She resolved to send slides of the triangles to a few London galleries. It would give her some idea whether it was worth carrying on. She began mentally writing an accompanying letter.

To Cath's surprise, Alecto International no less, asked her to bring the triangles to them. Packing a selection, she set off for her appointment with a fluttering heart. She couldn't believe this could really be a breakthrough. She was right. Ushered into a boardroom, a small dark man lounged at the end of a highly polished table. He languidly watched her unwrap the triangles, murmuring

'I see...'. She hurriedly arranged them in chevrons and hexagons, explaining

'This is just the start. I'm planning to cover the whole spectrum eventually.'

He interrupted her flow, and, breaking up the arrangements, he told her why he had wanted to see them. He was looking for a triangular logo, to promote his exhibitions in a large London store.

'But these are unsuitable' was his verdict.

With a dismissive wave at Cath and the triangles, he swiftly departed from the room.

Though despondent, she decided to try a few galleries on Bond Street. In one of them, a pleasant faced youth asked to see the triangles. As she unpacked them and put one or two on the counter, the owner arrived.

'Get those out of here!' he snarled.

Picking them up unwrapped, he practically threw them into her trolley. He wheeled it out at speed, slamming the door on the intruder. Further encounters proved equally sterile. Cath returned home stripped of her illusion. Success in new art was impossible for a housewife. Buying a London paper, she turned to the Situations Vacant.

The following day, she was to be interviewed for a fashion sketching job, in London's East End. She travelled on three trains before reaching the place. Through streets of small shops and old brick built factories, the name Fenkelstein sprang into sight. Its large letters spread along a shabby looking building, not more than twenty years old. Without much enthusiasm she entered, taking a lift to the third floor.

As the doors opened, an excitement gripped her. Repartee flashed at a Marx Brothers speed. A scimitar sharp profile turned, Groucho brows above an insolent smile. The smiler advanced to the open door, his arm around Cath as he ushered her in. If this was harassment, it was far from unpleasant, speeding its thrill through her veins.

'I'm Jake, costings,' the cutter went on, 'and this is Peter, head cutter.'

Peter was tall and blond, his trousers slung below a belly. Looking around, Cath vaguely registered other heads, bent over piles of patterns. On Jake and Peter's benches, patterns were laid on colourful cloth, with a nearby desk for the sketcher. Stroking Jake's bench, Peter grinned

'You've got a good lay there Jake!' he said, winking and glancing at Cath.

Designer Matt Goldberg joined them. When they'd seen Cath's portfolio, the job was hers.

That weekend being fine, Cath persuaded a reluctant Alan to go out. Though earning a decent salary again, his fear of another redundancy cast a pall over things. The high spirits Cath had felt through the drive ebbed away, in the tea-room of a National Trust property.

'Just look at the prices!' Alan loudly remarked. 'They've got to pay for the upkeep of the place' Cath murmured, 'Its worth paying extra for good food and surroundings.' 'If you've got someone else's pocket to dip into!' Alan sneered. The bitter tones destroyed what remained of Cath's pleasure. As they chose food, she pulled out her purse. 'Right, I'll pay!' she snapped, slamming the money on the counter. 'I won't have to beg for every penny now I'm working.'

Anxiously, Mark and Vanessa downed the last crumbs, avoiding Alan's sarcasm at left over food. As they all wandered through the rooms of the great house, Cath thought of the economies she'd made. Sunday joints replaced by stuffed hearts and stews. No new clothes since they'd moved. Thank goodness for her job.

Late that evening on the four seater settee, Cath moved closer to Alan.
Quickly moving away, he joked 'It's a pity I can't say to my footman 'James, titillate her ladyship tonight! I haven't got the energy myself.'
Though she laughed, she was sick of having to make overtures. She recalled a dream Alan had mentioned. In it, he was walking down the aisle with his white clad bride. In an instant, the sweet fresh virgin turned into a whore, loathsomely flaunting her over ripe charms.

Cath stepped into the factory lift on her first day at work. Matt the designer showed her the ropes. Pushing two discarded sketches into a waste bin, she began on her third. This time she hoped, the sketch had the ridiculously long limbs they wanted.

'That's more like it', Matt smiled encouragingly, 'In fact its' just what we want. Jake'll write in the trimmings for you, then you can have a go at this one.'

As he spoke, he began a rough sketch of a collar and cuffs.

Jake's nearness, his brushing of Cath's arm as he wrote, drew an answering fire. Her cheeks reddened as she saw Peter watching her, grinning as he worked.

'Jake's married with two kids you know.', he warned.

At lunch time, she dashed out to a corner shop and bought herself a square of bread and butter pudding. Spicy and strange, it seemed redolent of the whole new scene. As the weeks passed, she felt more at home among these 'displaced persons'. She was hardly surprised one lunch time when a small black child called

'Yiddisher!', as she passed in the street.

Peter sometimes talked of his concentration camp years. Freed at fourteen, he had wandered around Europe, finally ending up in a monastery. It had taken months to tell the monks he was Jewish, but he'd found sympathy when he confessed. Some days Peter sank into a depression, hardly speaking at all. There were undertones at the place that unnerved Cath, though she tried to appear blase. Odd people would call, like the rep selling buttons. He would chat to the men for hours.

Fragments such as 'Still on the game' would cause Cath a momentary unease.

Sometimes Alan seemed suspicious, as Cath talked of goings on at Fenkelstein's.

'You're always on about Peter and all these reps, but this Jake character?' You never mention what he gets up to.'

'Well he doesn't say much.' Cath blushed.

'It's what he does, not what he says that worries me.' Alan answered, searching her downturned face.

A lovely looking female rep would drop in, getting the Groucho eye from Jake. On one of her visits, he produced some tatty looking photos. Glancing at them, Cath first noticed the edges, in points as if cut with pinking shears. Looking again, she hid her surprise. Naked women took centre stage. Penises were in there, but disembodied, identifying details excluded. The paper, embossed with dots, gave a turn of the century look to the prints. Stifling doubts about Jake, Cath kept her eyes on her work.

One evening, the family sat down to one of Alan's well-cooked meals, he being home earliest now. He seemed quiet and pre-occupied. Cath didn't remark on it, he was so touchy these days, but at last he spoke.

'It's happened!' he said, 'I'm redundant again.'

'I'm sorry' Cath murmured inadequately, then rushed in with 'You should soon get some other work down here.'

Alan spoke again

'There's a possibility of a job in the North East. How would you feel about that?'

She hated the thought of it. Back to the land of no opportunity. Still, she'd be out of temptation's way where Jake was concerned. She reluctantly agreed. Alan got the job, living in the caravan temporarily.

Jake became more persuasive, when Cath let slip that Alan was away. His arm around her, he brought out a photo of a room, whispering
'How about a few hours with me here?'
Cath stiffened. The print had the same pinked edges as the pornographic photos she had seen. What was she getting involved in? Catching sight of Matt, Jake hurriedly put the photo away.
'If you're not careful Jake, you'll end up in the divorce court' Matt censured.
He carried on 'I couldn't do that myself. I've got too much respect for my wife.'
Jake reddened and they all fell silent.

On her return journey, Cath bought a local paper and found surprisingly, an ad for women artists near home. Taking a day off, she landed a job there, along with a weird looking group. They were to work on glass topped military style tables. With screen printed original drawings on one side, they would paint on the reverse. Seeing copies of Cath's fashion sketches, Crawford the employer enthused
'These are brilliant! I'd like you to do our original line drawings.'
The other women would colour the back of the glass to her colourings. Cath was thrilled, though the pay was poor. She finally gave notice at Fenkelstein's, though she missed the cutting room camaraderie.

That night she had a dream. She stood on a grassy bank, gazing into the scintillating waters of a pool. The sun poured down to meet the heady scents of its luxurious shores. It seemed natural and lovely to dive into its sun shot depths, until she saw a figure at its outer edge. Her mother-in-law's gnarled finger pointed, witch like, as venom snaked from her lips. Cath abruptly woke into a cold world, where Jake had to be forgotten.

Next Monday, Cath started work at Britannia International. She clocked in at a time-clock, for the first time for years. Though some women worked flexi hours, Cath felt she must work full time to supervise. In a bare room with a concrete floor, Roy Crawford showed them how to colour the glass. First brushing in details, he then deftly dabbed in backgrounds with a cotton wool pad. Land sea and sky glowed into life. Many of the prints were blow ups of old maps, though some were from original drawings. Cath felt well able to cope with the line drawings, when Crawford proudly claimed to be the artist of a clumsily drawn glass.

The women were each given a glass to work on, soon stopping for coffee from a machine. A heavy faced girl introduced herself as Val, just blown in from Tunisia. She had been singing with a pop group out there. The others were slim Mona, around twenty, and smart fortyish Ruth. As they finished their drinks, a young woman entered the room in a powered wheelchair. On his way out, Crawford whispered,

'I couldn't refuse her a job, poor bitch.'

Named Sandra, she had driven herself over in a mini-van, and was to work there only in the mornings.

As week followed week, Cath loved the work and the company. Val's Tunisian nights' entertainments were rich, rivalled by Mona's marital hang ups. Ruth, at first too shocked to laugh, came round. Sandra, a car accident victim, had set a precedent at Stoke Mandeville. She hadn't had post accident depression. Witty and sharp, she drove the girls out in her mini van for lunch. Here, Cath could speak of a past she had kept quiet for years.

The children had had school dinners since they'd moved. Vanessa made something on toast for their tea. Mark's job was to put a match to the fire. Now, working near home, Cath could care for them herself. Years later, Vanessa confessed that mild seeming Mark had been a pyromaniac. Undoing some of Cath's rolled papers, he would light them and float them up the chimney!

With the cracks in the ancient chimney, it was miraculous there'd been only one fire. Cath remembered it well. Red hot soot had poured into the fireplace, while smoke and flames shot skywards. Flying to the studio, Alan had brought down a huge metal plate, pushing it under the grate until the fire brigade arrived.

On one of his weekends at home, Alan had seemed preoccupied.
'What's on your mind Love?' Cath ventured.
Alan broke out 'If you want to know, I was wondering how you could fancy that Yiddisher tailor. He looks like a lorry driver's mate.' Suddenly chilled, Cath cried
'How on earth do you know what he looked like?' He was a thing of the past to her now, if not so to Alan.
'You didn't know did you? On your last day I had some time off and drove to the factory. Three of you were just coming out, finishing off the cream cakes you'd bought. I followed you to the pub, then turned round and drove home. I still can't see why you didn't leave sooner.'
'I've left now. Let's forget it.' Cath answered, but she knew it wouldn't be easy.

Some weeks later their house was on the market. Alan begged Cath 'Please let's have Mum here, until we find a place with a granny flat.' He was practically in tears. Wrung with guilt, Cath had to say
'No. It could be a year before we move. I just couldn't stand it! I'd be eating stewed cabbage in the mental home here!'
She meant every word. Alan didn't mention it again until Christmas, but it distanced them more from each other.

In the North East Alan began looking for a house. Months dragged on, he had found nothing suitable and not a buyer was in sight for their present home. Though Cath had loved the Coach House, she would be glad to see the back of its hazards, the cracked chimney, the worm-eaten floor and the open rail. Eventually, Alan found a suitable house in Hexham with a grannie flat, and an estate agent found a buyer for their Sussex home.

Alan had fetched his mother for Christmas As she stepped from the car, her swollen feet in their Minnie Mouse shoes were less sprightly. Her face looked drawn and her eyes had a vacant stare. The family sat down to a salad tea. Later they were having a good-bye party. Avoiding the gaze of the skeletally thin figure at the table, Cath felt an unwelcome hate. Through the meal, it hardened like cooling lava. She tried to evoke sympathy for the old lady, but could not.

For the party, Cath wore an ankle length skirt, made for her by Val. Its woven art deco design was in brown black and gold.

She brushed on her mascara in front of the dining room mirror. Her bright eyes and racing heart signalled that the ephedrine was having its effect. It was some time since she had taken the drug, now that soberer treatments were in use. She had found an old bottle and thought they might pep up the evening.

Shuffling feet made her turn, as Alan and his mother came into the room. Looking into the glass, she saw, mirrored, the furious face of her mother-in-law. Then the mother exclaimed

'Who's that woman ? That frightful woman!', as she stared at Cath's reflected image.

Alan glanced wordlessly at Cath, as he turned and led the frail figure out. 'The poor thing's flipped.' Cath thought. Chilled by more than cold weather, she threw on a shawl.

As the guests began arriving, she put on records of the Beatles and Stones. Pouring out drinks, she handed one to Sandra. Sitting beside her wheelchair, she watched Mona and Val dance to an already nostalgic Sergeant Pepper. The Hippie era was drifting to its' close. Seeing Alan only at weekends, she had grown fond of her weekday life with the women. A little more ephedrine heightened her mood, as she too, joined in the dance. Avidly they ate old style bridge rolls and trifle. Not for Cath the dips of women's magazines. Later, through an ephedrine-alcohol daze, she saw a multi coloured rain. Someone had flung trifle at the lowered pine ceiling. By now she neither knew nor cared who. Alan, practical as ever, brought a bucket of water and a stepladder. The trifle thrower stumbled through the lobby, passing out behind the front door!

Returning home to Manchester after Christmas, Alan's mother finally succumbed to senility. Neighbours found her wandering the streets, in the early hours of a frosty morning. She was shrieking repeatedly

'Alan! Where's Alan?'

They had her placed in a residential home, the impossibility of the granny flat now clear. Visiting her there, she smiled excitedly, saying

'Alan's coming today!'

'I am Alan!' her son exclaimed, but sadly, she didn't know him.

In the now too large house in Hexham, months turned into years. Alan enjoyed his new management work. Eventually, life became hectic for Cath, with free-lance work and printing plus graphics at a party plan company. Then her clear vision began to fail.

Chapter 20

This Eighties year, Cath, tall siblings Vanessa and Mark, plus a reluctant Alan, had had a stall at one or two craft fairs. Vanessa sold her jewellery and Mark his photographic panoramas. Cath displayed her litho prints, her 'Cloned' series and a number of small local views. This coming Saturday, they were to sell their work at a more exciting venue, the 'Festival of the Air'. They looked forward to the display of fantasy kite flying, put on by the Japanese promoters.

The festival began with a downpour, but clearing skies brought the crowds. The crafts were in one of three vast marquees. Though the continuous promenade grew, few seemed to linger at the Robbs' stall. Normally Vanessa's earrings were a strong attraction. Created from feathers brilliant and subtly natural, or glass scintillating under spotlights, they usually caught the eye. Here, a too small generator prevented the use of individual lighting. Only three lamps, at intervals along the marquee's ridge, added to rare sunlight. Discouraged, Vanessa burst out

'You can hardly see our stuff Mum!'

'All this kitsch around won't help.' Mark added, but he sold two panoramas before lunch.

Next to the Robb's stall was one covered with plastic grass, featuring a plethora of garden gnomes. These, Cath assumed, were cast in bought moulds and painted in quantity, by the stallholder and outworkers. The scarlet hats could be seen from the marquee entrance, attracting crowds of buyers. Cath stared at the jolly little faces, more cloned than her illustrated twins and so much more in demand.

A toy maker had taken the right hand stall. Among soft toys, the starkly black faces of gollywogs stood out. There were females as well as the minstrel style males.

'Are these popular with black kids?' Cath asked.

'You'd be surprised,' the woman answered, 'the first one I made was for a black nurse. I was making Victorian dolls and she asked me to make a black one. I made one of these gollies and she loved it! I've made them ever since. I don't make the white ones any more, because these sell so much better.'

Cath smiled, her eyes lingering on the gollies. She remembered them from her childhood, but these were particularly inhuman. Their tufted hair, round eyes and curling clown mouths seemed hallucinatory.

Mark sold another panorama and Vanessa plenty of jewellery. Occasionally, an appreciative eye would linger over the 'Cloned' series.

'Look at these!' an elderly man said to his wife.

After carefully reading the captions, he remarked

'They're strange......'

Disappointingly, he wandered away, though after picking up a price list and card.

Encouraged by a TV programme, featuring a Victorian silhouettist, Cath had brought pads of black and white paper. After hanging up a notice 'SILHOUETTES £1.50 WHILE YOU WAIT', she began a silhouette of her daughter. Mounted on white, it looked reasonable and, intrigued, Vanessa decided to try herself. Deft twists and turns of the scissors soon produced a brilliantly lifelike image of her father. With its beard and curve of the nose, the cut out head had a handsome remoteness familiar to Cath. Looking at it, she regretted that this distance of his flashed into animation with others, not herself these days. Soon they were getting a number of subjects, mother and daughter taking it in turns. Before long, they had used up the whole of the pads, but were far from making much money, compared to neighbouring stalls.

In slacker periods, one or other would wander off to join the kite flying throng outside. For sale in the Japanese tent were inconceivable kinds of kite. On display in the air were spectacular specimens, most notably 'The Legs'. These were shorts, their training-shoed limbs floating weightless. Another favourite was the many hued cone, its helical stripes endlessly rotating. Traditional kites were also airborne, recalling to Cath the woodcut waves of Hokusai. With an intensity beyond realism, sword swinging samurai snarled. Frog-eyed fiends haunted the wind torn sky. Also on sale were toy-like miniature trees. Beside them, flower arrangements each had a twisting branch, its claw like curves alive with ancient dragon rhythms.

On the Sunday, the family were relaxing with TV and papers. Cath decided on a walk. The weather continued windy, the sky an intense blue between racing clouds. She struggled up a steep hill. As she approached a stone faced terrace, she saw, on the hill's brow, the house with the Chinese garden. Eagerly she remembered its strange carved blocks. Coming closer, seeing its trimmed shrubbery, she recalled the dark quarry further round the hill. As she skirted the curving garden wall, a 'FOR SALE' sign caught her eye. A sudden excitement at the vague thought of buying the place was quickly dashed as front lawns came fully into view. The quivering limbs and dilate eyes of the oriental beasts were gone. Their plinths remained. Stolidly centred on each, was a red capped garden gnome.......

Propelled by curiosity, Cath ventured up the winding path. Answering the doorbell, an elderly man peered suspiciously over his glasses, but as Cath expressed her interest, he invited her in. He explained that he was ignorant of the garden sculptures' origins.

'They were there when I bought the place thirty years ago.'
he told her.

A widower, he would move into a residential home when he'd sold up. Photos of him and his wife stood out among the art deco artefacts that filled every available space. They were childless it seemed.

When Cath enquired again about the stone pieces now missing from their plinths, the man replied

'I've sold them to a Hexham antique shop for five hundred pounds.'

This sounded far less than they were actually worth. As Cath thanked him and left, a mood of despondency swept over her. The bright sun now sank behind deepening clouds. She didn't look back at the hill top house. Its magic had vanished with its attendant beasts.

Back at the hospital, Cath again passed through the hothouse corridors on her way to more laser treatment. She was glad of Alan's help in finding Pavilion 2, its wavering sign being so hard to see. After drops dilated her eye, the thud of the laser shot through her skull. The young specialist's talk had been short at Cath's visit on her own. He now explained an elaborate diagram, addressing Alan, though he knew less of medicine than Cath. The result of the treatment seemed good, apart from the lacing of burnt capillaries. Hopefully loss of focusing had been stemmed in that eye.

About seven p.m., some weeks later, Cath was on her way to meet members of the Hanover Press. Publicity shots were to be taken at a Metro station. As she passed through the turnstiles at St. James's station, she hoped the others would soon be there. The place was unnerving. Tiled from floor to ceiling like an immense urinal, its escalator disappeared in subterranean gloom. Thankfully she saw Roy Clement, his glasses reflecting bright points of light. Then Sheena and Mike arrived with newer members. The local press took photos of them on the escalator, with Cath, the smallest, in front.

They completed the shooting early, fortunately as it turned out. The group were on their way to the Bridge Hotel. On the bank of the Tyne, the pub was shadowed by one of the bridges. At this point, alarmingly, buildings, signs and street lamps began to waver before Cath's eyes. The treatment hadn't worked after all....... She decided to go with them to the pub, saying nothing. They sat drinking outside in the fading light and warmth. As they talked, the group's faces took on a Cubist geometry. The cast iron supports of the nearby bridge reeled dizzily or crumpled in zigzag waves.

'Can I give you a lift home?' Sheena asked, 'I'm going your way.'

Worried about negotiating the roads, Cath eagerly accepted. As flies zoomed around the tables she sat still, seeing a bleak future ahead.

Next morning, her heart racing, Cath took a taxi to the eye department. She found a seat among the crowd for her interminable wait. Looking around she noticed with a curious detachment, small objects, door handles, ashtrays, appear and disappear. Closing each eye in turn, she saw that the right eye's sight was poorer than the left. She wondered if the laser had actually added to the overall damage.

She leafed through a magazine, reading only the titles. The consultant told her nothing more could be done.

'The laser treatment was only temporary,' he said, 'but we hoped it might last a few years.'

Given an impression that it might last for life, Cath was choked into a dumb acceptance.

Discharged from Eye Outpatients, Cath waited alone. Recalled to the present by the sound of her name, she claimed the magnifying glasses on frames. With them she could read large print, though incredibly slowly. It seemed hardly worthwhile. Cassette books would be easier. She refused the white wand and dark glasses. She felt they would confuse drivers and bring unwanted help. Stepping out into the glare of the sun, she found that by waiting until roads were empty, she could cross safely. She must keep her self reliance. Getting off her bus, the curving street lamps were unnerving. Later this distortion would disappear, leaving a manageable blurring. Staff never told her this, though it would have helped a lot.

She awoke next morning to a sickening awareness of her distorted world. As Alan rushed for his nominal wash, she saw her two paintings with a lurch of the heart. Frames sagged or zigzagged, their contents beyond recognition. She got breakfast without problems, though her coffee almost spilled. Reaching for the paper, she recalled that she could only read headlines.

In her studio room she picked up an airbrush piece almost completed. It was the first in a series commissioned by a London print company. She pushed it aside. Seeing it as blurred and distorted, she could never finish it or the series now. As all meaning seemed stripped from her world, she dialled the RNIB. No-one answered. It wasn't yet nine. Alan, unable to find words, had left early for work. As he opened the front door, Cath had noticed the greyness of his hair and beard. She regretted that they hadn't been closer...... Her reverie was cut short by the braking of the minibus from the party plan company, where she worked part time. She took her seat, and on arrival, handed in her notice to the new office manager.

Recently promoted and eager to avoid problems, he said nothing to others about Cath.

'Don't give up yet.' he advised Cath, 'Just carry on and see how it goes.'

Stalling for time, she agreed and found that she could still print the stationery, helped by her magnifying glasses. All morning she experimented and by evening had decided to take back her notice. The manager's relief at the finished newsletter was plain. An artistic junior from the office took over the graphics. Cath still had something to hang on to. The precipice had receded a few feet.

At home, her mind returned to causes of her vision loss. She recalled the packed lunches in Hanover Square gardens. Dog parasites could affect the eyes. Or could anti depressives be responsible. Unexplained nose bleeds had happened when the eye bleeds began. Could it be some other cure, the ephedrine she had taken for years? Could this strange drug, changing lethargy to excitement, have its drawbacks? Why had it faded from the medical scene? She couldn't regret the highs. Like Cocteau's heroin, it had given her perfect hours.

Cath's thoughts wandered to her graphics course thesis, on drug influences on art. She had read that ephedrine was in soma, an ancient Indian hallucinogen, known as 'The drink that makes us see the Gods.' Could this explain their many limbed deities? Researching, she had read between the lines, from erudite art books to Timothy Leary.

In Leary's accounts of acid trips, Paisley shapes swirled around Hi Fi's and curled from the lips of his friends. This fired Cath's curiosity about the strange shapes. Similar swirls flowed from faces in Aztec art books, plainly the same as in Paisley prints. These were first copied from Indian imports, then printed by the million in Paisley Scotland, hence the name.

Cath also recalled the eye dilation of the Chinese dragons. These ball-eyed beasts often stared from temple corners, in the four directions, to protect from evil spirits. They appeared again in Aztec and Mayan art. The same fearful intensity of eye and mouth, in the form of a mask, was also carved on the gateways of Indian temples. Her art books termed it 'The Face of Glory'.

For Cath, De Quincey's account of an opium experience had thrown more light on Chinese art. From his lakeside view, heightened peaks rose over infinite space. Below, lake shores became vast savannahs. The words recalled silk-drawn Chinese scenes, in which fragile temples hung over infinite space. When forming a long unwinding scroll, these landscapes expanded time as well as space. The tiny figures had, for Cath, a ripeness seldom seen in posturing Western oils. In these, an earth centred universe existed for the benefit of mankind, or was it men?

Cath remembered how she had placed her finished thesis in two leafed folders. On each honey coloured binding was a square of paisley in iridescent tones, echoing its coloured pages. Her fantasy water-colours and photocopies of drug induced art almost completed the project. Her last step was to add gold-leafed lettering and corner motifs.

The meeting in bookbinding, with two girls from the fashion department, was an eye-opener. An odd couple, she had seen them wandering around in their afghans, hardly speaking to others. Having asked about Cath's work, one of them had remarked

'Are you sure you know what you're talking about Man? We've tried it all - mushrooms, acid, the lot!'

'Mushrooms are the best!' the other had added.

She had imaged the incredible beauty of the stars, after the mushroom drink. She had gone on to describe an LSD terror trip, dragging her screaming friend on to a bus. In Lewis Caroll fashion, the bus had appeared shrunk to the size of a toy. The screamer was almost trapped in its doors.

Cath had regretted being unable to use these revelations in her thesis, the closing date being next day. Again in the present, she determined to use her new magnifying glasses to carry on with her prints.

Next morning, the persistent ring of the ancient alarm finally became solid reality. The horns and pan pipes of a dream lingered in memory for some time. Grabbing a pad, Cath hastily recaptured its scenes for her psychology class. Later they would deal with the interpretation of dreams. This morning's dream began with a walk past hedgerows and summer trees. At a cross-roads, a sign showed her the way, but a group of men, strong, earthy, barred her. They glanced contemptuously down. Seeing that argument was useless, Cath chose another route.

Turning a corner, she saw a scene of visionary splendour. Along a valley floor were beings lit by a strange radiance. The central group, all men, were each balanced on a geometric form, cube, sphere and cylinder. Grecian garments flowed to their feet. Around them men and women danced, their shining wreathes intensifying the great light. Cath longed to be with them, as the piercing beauty of pan pipes and horns dissolved into the morning alarm.

While writing the dream down for her class, Cath felt details were slipping away, though it was unlikely the lecturer would want to hear more. Generally, he welcomed neither questions nor comments, and few besides her offered either.

Recently, he had spoken of findings that a part of the brain concerned with the emotions was larger in females than in males. Cath with unusual speed had snapped back 'Does this apply to the female ape?'

'I haven't heard of any such work' he had replied, adding, clinically cool eye flashing, 'You've got an answer for everything!'

However, though she expected some caustic comment on the dream, she decided to keep it on file.

The last psychology class, on dreams, was also the tutor's own assessment. Dreams were now to be last on the agenda. Cath decided on a recurring dream, feeling the visionary glade would be too long. She told of scaling an immense Victorian frontage in Harold Lloyd style. A longing to enter a window above, drove her on. The music and laughter, the lamplight streaming through coloured panes seemed unattainable. Interrupting her to remark

'Oh that's the old one of the infant climbing the mother to reach the breast.' the tutor swiftly turned to the next anxious dreamer.

His casual remark might be the answer to her search for a future, Cath mused. Could she express in words the lives of the twins? Could the essence of memory be distilled?